THE JADE TURTLE

When Jack and Alice split up, he broke not only her heart, but also their business partnership. Running their agency alone, Alice discovers that Lan Nguyen had, unbeknownst to her, contracted Jack to steal a jade turtle. Unable to refund Lan, Alice is expected to take on the job herself. Reluctant to commit theft, she finds an unexpected ally in Jack's brother Mike. Then somebody else steals the turtle first — and Alice and Mike must find out who!

MARGARET MOUNSDON

THE JADE TURTLE

Complete and Unabridged

LINFORD
Leicester

First published in Great Britain in 2019

First Linford Edition
published 2020

A catalogue record for this book is available
from the British Library.

ISBN 978–1–4448–4525–9

Published by
Ulverscroft Limited
Anstey, Leicestershire

Set by Words & Graphics Ltd.
Anstey, Leicestershire
Printed and bound in Great Britain by
T. J. International Ltd., Padstow, Cornwall

This book is printed on acid-free paper

Impossible Request

'Who are you?' Lan spoke with the crisp precision of someone whose first language was not English.

The peacock blue of Lan Nguyen's high-collared tea gown shimmered as a ray of sun caught the delicate weave of the slub silk. Alice took several deep breaths, wishing she had re-thought her own outfit of black leggings and damp polo shirt.

'Alice Fairfax.'

'And why are you here?'

Alice took another deep breath.

'I came to explain that Jack Preston and I have parted company and that I won't be able to fulfil whatever professional arrangement he had with you.'

Alice could feel drops of rain sliding off her hair and down the back of her shirt. She didn't want to shiver but she couldn't help herself.

'Do you have a respiratory problem?' Lan enquired as Alice did her best to get her breath back.

'The lift is out of action,' she explained, 'and the rain made me late. Did you see the rainbow? I always think they are so beautiful.' She knew her tongue was running away with her. It always did when she was stressed.

'And you say Mr Preston isn't joining us?' Lan ignored the reference to rainbows.

'I'm afraid not.'

'Where is he?'

'He's otherwise engaged,' Alice replied, wishing she had the answer to that question herself.

'And you are unaware of the details of any arrangement I had with Mr Preston?'

'That's right.'

'He is the senior partner in your agency?'

'We're equal partners,' Alice said with firm insistence, 'or rather, we were.'

'Why should I believe you when you say you know nothing of Mr Preston's affairs?'

'Because I am not in the habit of lying.' Alice spoke with more intensity than was perhaps wise when dealing with a potential client.

'Equal partners share responsibility, don't they?' Lan Nguyen enquired in a calm voice.

How Ms Nguyen could remain so cool in this complex situation Alice had no idea but she was determined to match her dignity.

'I kept this appointment,' Alice spoke slowly and carefully, anxious not to betray more emotion than was necessary, 'because in your e-mail you asked for an update on Jack's progress.'

'That is correct.'

'I came to tell you I was kept in the dark on this. I am sorry if you choose not to believe me but that's the truth.'

'And have you also come to return the advance?'

'What advance?' Alice demanded, a

nasty jolt working its way up her spine.

'I paid Mr Preston a substantial advance. If he is not going to fulfil his obligation I would like my money back.'

'Can I sit down?' Alice asked as her legs threatened to buckle underneath her.

Lan paused then inclined her head in acknowledgement.

'You would perhaps like a cup of green tea to refresh yourself,' she offered, 'while we discuss this matter?'

'Thank you.'

Alice sank gratefully on to a hard-backed wooden chair and watched Lan prepare the tea. The scent of lotus flowers transported her back to the South China Sea and the idyllic island she and Jack had visited on their holiday cruise. What a fool she had been to trust him.

Lan placed a minuscule teacup in front of Alice then sat down on the opposite side of the desk and began tapping on her keyboard while Alice sipped her tea.

'You are finished?' Lan asked a few moments later, not looking up from her laptop.

'Yes. Thank you.'

Alice nudged the fragile teacup away from the edge of Lan's desk. It could be valuable and she didn't want to add unnecessary breakages to her mounting debts.

'Good.' Lan swung back to face her.

Alice found it difficult to guess her age. She had a smooth complexion and high cheekbones and dark brown eyes that were so deep in colour they were almost black. The silk dress clung in all the right places and emphasised her petite figure. Her hair was tied back in a neat bun. Never had Alice felt so clumsy and gauche.

'Did Mr Preston tell you anything about the jade turtle?' Lan asked.

Alice could hear the swish of car tyres racing down the road outside that ran alongside the derelict industrial estate. There had been rumours that the site of the old brick works had been sold for development but nothing had come of them and occasionally the premises were used for photo shoots or team building days.

Alice assumed Lan had leased one of the offices on a temporary basis. All the same, it was a strange place to conduct business of a delicate nature, which she presumed this assignment was.

'No,' Alice replied to Lan's question, 'Mr Preston told me nothing at all about you.'

'Then if you would be good enough to return my advance I will look elsewhere for assistance.'

Alice gulped.

'I can't,' she admitted.

'You cannot do what?'

'Return your advance.'

The office was growing stuffy and Alice longed for some fresh air but the skylight looked as though it hadn't been opened in a long time.

'Why not?' Lan asked.

'I don't have it.'

The agency had been operating on a

shoestring and any profit had been ploughed back into the business. Any unexpected expense would take them well above their overdraft limit and Alice had already had more than one challenging interview with the bank.

'In that case,' Lan spoke with such cold precision Alice knew there was no chance she would change her mind, 'you leave me with no choice.'

'Please don't involve the police,' Alice implored. Lan looked startled by her outburst. 'I'll find some way to pay you back but I have to have time.'

Lan looked hard at Alice then seemed to come to a decision.

'If you cannot return the money you will have to take Jack Preston's place.'

'Doing what?' Alice hardly dared ask the question.

'You will steal the jade turtle for me.'

'What?' Alice almost shrieked.

'I'll give you forty-eight hours to think about it.'

'What jade turtle?' Alice pleaded.

'Forty-eight hours, Ms Fairfax. Now

if you will excuse me, I have a busy morning.'

More Bad News

From the warmth of the steamy café Alice watched rain bounce off the pavement. Her espresso cooled on the table in front of her.

Jack Preston's brother was absolutely the last person in this world who would lift a finger to help her. She wasn't even sure he was going to turn up but she had no-one else to turn to.

She had no idea what devil-may-care Jack had got himself into now but it sounded like trouble — serious trouble and as head of the family Mike could sort it out.

Alice's father had done casual gardening work for the Prestons when Alice had been a child and during the summer holidays she had occasionally joined him, helping to weed the vegetable patch.

She remembered seeing Mike and

Jack's mother sitting under a spreading beech tree wearing a huge hat and floaty summer dress, sipping lemonade and dispensing slices of fruitcake. Major Preston drove a fast car and was always too busy to talk to anyone. In those days she recalled the sun always seemed to shine.

Today's weather suited Alice's mood. Gunmetal grey clouds refused to budge. It had been raining steadily since breakfast — not that Alice had been in the mood to eat anything. Since the split with Jack her appetite had deserted her.

She jumped as droplets of water landed on her notebook. Startled, she looked up. Mike Preston was standing in front of her.

Alice felt a rush of blood to her head and her heartbeat tripled. She'd have to choose her words carefully or Mike would probably accuse her of inventing the whole thing in an attempt to discredit his brother. Family unity was the name of the game when it came to dealing with the Prestons.

Mike dabbed his dripping hair with a paper serviette that someone had left on another table. He reminded Alice of a shaggy dog emerging from a swim in the sea as he gave his head a final shake. Screwing up the serviette into a soggy ball he lobbed it into the recycling bin before turning his attention to Alice.

'Hi.'

The corner of his eyes crinkled into a smile that did nothing to reduce the rate of Alice's heartbeat. She swallowed and wished Mike didn't resemble his brother quite so much. Both Prestons possessed bucket-loads of charisma. They only had to walk into a room for all heads to turn their way.

'Have you been here long?' Without waiting for her to reply Mike flashed a smile at the barista who had emerged from behind the counter to close the door that had blown open from the force of the gale outside. 'Two espressos, please.'

He pulled out a chair and sat down opposite Alice.

'Hello, Mike,' she managed to say in the coolest possible voice. 'How are you?'

'You've lost weight.' He frowned.

'Is it any surprise?' Alice challenged.

'Perhaps not,' Mike acknowledged with a shamefaced smile.

The barista carried a tray of fresh brewed coffee over to their table, casting Alice an envious glance. Mike smiled his thanks. Although he wasn't as good-looking as his brother Jack, he knew how to use his charm and the barista looked ready to obey his every command. Mike spooned two tea-spoons of sugar into his cup and stirred thoughtfully.

'Sorry I wasn't in touch earlier but I signed out of my social media accounts for a week.'

'It doesn't matter, you're here now.'

Mike appeared not to have heard Alice's comment. He carried on stirring his coffee.

'You may as well hear it from me,' he said.

Alice suppressed a weary sigh.

'Hear what?' Over the past few weeks she had heard enough bad news to last a lifetime.

Mike took a deep breath.

'Jack . . . ' he stalled.

'Yes?' Alice encouraged.

'He's married.'

Alice waited for the blinding flash of pain to stab her in the ribs.

'Sorry to be the one to break the news,' Mike said, mistaking her gasp of surprise for one of dismay.

Alice saw no reason to enlighten him. When it came to Jack Preston she had no reserves of emotion left.

'Last week,' Mike continued when there was no further reaction from Alice.

'Last week?' Alice kept her voice neutral.

'I was best man.'

Alice grimaced as she sipped her cooling coffee. She wished Mike wouldn't keep looking at her so intently.

'Viv Hollingsworth?' Alice enquired.

Mike gave another uncomfortable smile. Viv Hollingsworth, Jack's ex, was the daughter of a successful business-man and a talented artist whose work was showcased in all the local galleries. She was also an heiress — a combina-tion Jack obviously found unable to resist.

Alice was relieved her own father had returned to his native Canada after the death of her mother. Of lumberjack stock with a keen interest in sport, Ken Fairfax might have been tempted to practise his boxing skills on Jack Preston had he still been living in Saltwich. It was from her father that Alice had inherited her height and sturdy limbs.

'Have you nothing to say?' Mike prompted.

'I've said all I'm going to say about Jack,' was Alice's firm and dignified reply.

'Perhaps it's for the best. Draw a line

under the past?'

'I'm not sure I can.'

'You wouldn't have suited,' Mike insisted.

'Meaning my father isn't chairman of a multi national corporation and I am not a talented heiress?' Alice tried and failed to keep the scorn out of her voice.

'Meaning exactly what I said. You weren't right for Jack.'

'Well, thank you for breaking the news.'

'I'm sorry he treated you so badly,' Mike said in such a soft voice that Alice's composure threatened to crumble.

'It wasn't apparent at the time.' Alice bit her lip. They were tiptoeing around dangerous territory. She needed Mike's help and she knew she would get nowhere by digging up the past.

'I . . . ' Mike started to explain.

'And you don't know the half of it.' Alice straightened her shoulders ready to get down to business.

Mike's blue eyes gave nothing away

as he looked at her. He downed his espresso in one gulp.

'That tasted good. I missed lunch. Think I'll order another.' He gestured to the barista. 'Anything for you?'

'No, thank you.'

'Then if you don't want to talk about Jack why are we here?'

'I need your help.'

Mike swivelled back to face her.

'My help?' he repeated in an incredulous voice.

Alice squirmed in her seat.

'Yes.'

'Things must be bad.'

Unable to think of a retort, Alice maintained her silence.

'Correct me if I'm wrong but I seem to recall the last time we met you said something along the lines of if you never saw me or Jack again it would be too soon.'

'Can you blame me? You stuck up for your brother.'

'There is such a thing as family loyalty.'

'Which Jack tested to its limit by running off with his old girlfriend.'

'So what's made you change your mind about seeing me again?' Mike cast an anxious glance over his shoulder as he changed the subject. 'Jack's not likely to gatecrash this little meeting, is he?'

'I meant what I said about Jack. I never want to see him again.'

'Why don't you tell me what this is all about,' Mike coaxed, 'and I promise I'll help if I can.'

The tone of his voice was so like Jack's it threatened to reduce Alice to a state of collapse.

'You're right. You can't help me.' She looked round for her bag. 'I'll pay for the coffee. I shouldn't have bothered you.'

'Not good enough.' Mike shook his head.

'Whatever happens, you are going to stick up for your brother, aren't you? Blood is thicker than water, especially when your name is Preston.'

'Look, you've dragged me halfway across town on the foulest day of the year.'

'Out of your nice warm office. It must be nice to have a comfortable office and a good job. I am so sorry to have disrupted your day.'

Mike ignored the jibe.

'You can't refuse to tell me why you're so anxious to see me.'

'I can do what I like and I'm better off going it alone. It's something I've got rather good at recently.'

'Stay where you are,' Mike ordered, snatching her bag out of her hands and placing it on the seat beside him and out of her reach.

'Hey,' Alice protested. 'Give it back.'

'I'm ravenous. It's a horrible day. Let's have a slice of lemon drizzle. You look like someone who missed out on lunch.' He signalled again to the hovering barista, 'Don't argue. The cakes are on me and no more talk about going solo or moving on.'

Alice lapsed into silence. The lemon

drizzle when it arrived was soft and gooey.

'You're not allowed to talk until you're finished,' Mike insisted, spooning up a healthy portion. 'And,' he added, 'no leaving any crumbs on the plate.'

Alice wiped her lips with the paper serviette.

'I never could win against you when it came to eating cake, could I?'

Feeling warm, Alice undid the knot of her leopard print scarf. One afternoon when Jack had stood her up for a reason that now escaped her memory, Mike had stepped in and entertained her to tea at a luxury hotel. He had been good company and teased her constantly about the number of strawberries she could eat in one sitting and the extra cakes she had asked to take home in a doggy bag.

Outside, the rain was easing and a tentative sun was doing its best to battle through the lowering clouds. Alice had forgotten how much she enjoyed Mike's company and with a full stomach she felt better placed to face the world.

'Now' — his eyes crinkled at the corners as he smiled — 'on you go. You have my full attention. What is this all about?'

Trouble Ahead?

'There are times when I could wring my little brother's neck.' Mike's forehead was creased in an angry frown after Alice finished telling him about Lan Nguyen.

'Can you get hold of him?' Alice pleaded, 'and ask about Lan and the advance she paid him?'

'Hold on a moment,' Mike held up a hand, 'we don't know this Lan person gave Jack an advance. It's only her word against his.'

'Why would she invent such a story?' Alice demanded.

'Stranger things have happened. You say there's no paper trail?'

'You're sticking up for Jack again, aren't you?' Alice gave an angry toss of her head. 'The rest of the world can be convinced your brother is guilty but not you.'

'Steady,' Mike cautioned. 'I'm trying to think things through here.'

'Can't you see this time Jack has got himself into something serious?'

'We haven't heard Jack's side of the story.'

'That's why we have to get hold of him.' Mike hesitated.

'It isn't going to be easy.'

'That doesn't surprise me.'

'He's on his honeymoon.'

'But you must know where he is.'

'I don't — exactly.'

'When will you stop being so stubborn and tell me where he is or do you want the police hammering on your door?' Alice was fast losing patience with Mike.

'Why should they hammer on my door?'

'Because you are Jack's next of kin and I won't have any hesitation in grassing you up should the need arise.'

'You've been watching too many police dramas.' There was the hint of a smile in Mike's voice. 'Have you no honour?'

'Not when it comes to taking the rap for something I haven't done.' Breathing heavily, Alice lapsed into silence.

'Have you finished?' Mike asked in a careful voice.

Alice nodded.

'Then listen up. Viv's father has chartered a private yacht and paid for an exclusive cruise in the Caribbean as a wedding present.'

'And that's supposed to make me feel better?'

'I'm doing my best here,' Mike insisted.

'Actually I can't say I blame Mr Hollingsworth,' Alice said.

'What's that remark supposed to mean?' Mike demanded.

'If Viv were my daughter newly married to Jack then sending them out to the Caribbean would seem like a good idea. I'm sure I'm not the only one who would like a quiet word with him.'

'He's not as bad as he's made out to be,' Mike insisted.

'I hope you're not going to spin me a tale about him being misunderstood as a child?'

'There may be an innocent explanation.'

'That's why we have to talk to him.'

'Like I said, it's not going to be easy.'

'He can't cut himself off completely,' Alice protested. 'What if there's an emergency?'

'Then I am to contact Viv's father.'

'And doesn't this class as an emergency? Jack has made off with money that is not rightfully his and is possibly involved in stealing a valuable artefact.'

'I understand what you're saying.'

'Then why won't you give me Mr Hollingsworth's number?'

'He won't put you through if he discovers your previous relationship with Jack.'

'Then I won't tell him.'

Mike shook his head.

'Mr Hollingsworth's a businessman, he'll demand details.'

Alice banged the table with the flat of her hand causing the barista to look up from her magazine in alarm.

'Couldn't you invent an emergency?'

Alice knew the moment she made the suggestion that from the expression on Mike's face it was a non-starter.

'That wouldn't be right.'

Occasionally there were times when Alice wondered how Jack and Mike Preston could be brothers, even if they stuck together like glue. Being five years younger than Mike Jack had been their mother's favourite and she had spoilt him outrageously. Whatever Jack wanted he got. Jack wouldn't have turned a hair at inventing a family emergency. Mike, it seemed, would.

'Then there's nothing you can do to help me, is there?' Alice accepted the inevitable. 'I'm wasting my time.'

'Not so fast.' Mike paused.

The barista hovered by their table.

'Would you like these?' She offered a

plate of dark chocolate mints. 'They're part of a local promotion.'

'That's it!' Mike almost knocked the plate out of the barista's hands. 'Thank you so much. These look delicious.'

He began unwrapping silver foil. The confused barista returned his smile and retreated to the safety of her counter.

'What was all that about?' Alice demanded.

'Here, have one of these,' Mike unwrapped a peppermint cream, 'while I explain.'

Alice nibbled absently on the dark chocolate whilst waiting for Mike to enlighten her.

'Before I went off to do my stint as Jack's best man I was overseeing the promotional literature for the arts festival. See?' He held up the embossed wrapping.

'This is one of your graphic designs?' Alice flushed, regretting her earlier taunt about Mike's career. He was a talented artist who had worked hard to get where he was.

Mike nodded.

'And how can this festival help us?' she asked.

'This year the Tao centre is playing host.'

Mike looked expectantly at Alice.

'Get to the point,' she urged.

'Jade,' Mike blurted out.

'What about it?'

'There's going to be a display of artwork in the centre and I'm sure amongst the paperwork there was reference to a turtle.'

'And you think this is the turtle Lan is referring to?'

'Don't you? I mean there can't be two jade turtles in Saltwich, can there? Our east coast community is hardly at the forefront when it comes to that sort of art.'

'And you think Jack was going to somehow acquire this turtle for Lan?'

'It's as good a place to start as any.'

'Exactly how do I start?' Alice demanded.

'You need to talk to David Liu.'

'I need to talk to Jack.'

'Start with David. See how you get on.'

Alice's head was buzzing.

'Jack can't seriously have considered stealing a jade turtle. He was always short of money but thieving would be a step too far even for him.'

'Can you come up with a better suggestion?'

'What if I call Lan's bluff?'

'And what if she goes to the police?'

The lemon drizzle churned in Alice's stomach.

'She can't prove anything.'

'Maybe not but are you willing to take the chance?'

'No,' Alice admitted in a hollow voice.

'Why on earth did you get involved with my brother?' Mike demanded.

'I suppose all this is my fault now?' Alice protested.

'That's not what I meant, but Jack and business do not mix. He lost most of our grandmother's inheritance on some ghastly financial venture.'

'That's why we set up together.'

'I never did quite figure out the nature of your business with him.'

'We were fixers.'

Mike raised an enquiring eyebrow.

'We walked dogs, watered plants, house sat, that sort of thing. We had plenty of introductions and the agency was doing well but any profit was ploughed back into the business. It was harder work than either of us envisaged.'

'I get the picture.'

'We operated from an office above the art studio complex in the precinct.'

'Number fifteen?'

'Do you know it?'

'It's part of the Preston portfolio.'

'You mean I am living in your flat?'

'You're still there?'

'I've nowhere else to go.'

'Jack did leave you in the lurch, didn't he?'

'At last I seem to be getting through

to you. You're not going to evict me, are you?'

Mike seemed not to hear her question.

'Do you know anything about jade?' he asked.

'It's a girl's name and isn't it green?'

'Not always. It can be green or black or purple.'

Alice looked out of the window. The rain had eased and sun was shining on a patch of spilled oil in the road creating a jade mosaic.

'Is that so?'

'It is also regarded as a protector of evil — and it can bring you the love you desire,' Mike added, looking faintly embarrassed.

'So that's where Jack and I went wrong.' Alice's lips twisted into a wry smile. 'We were short of jade.'

'You didn't do anything wrong,' Mike said.

He ran a hand through his hair, which was starting to dry.

'I am in the wrong,' Alice insisted, 'by

association if nothing else.'

'Jack was the one who walked out on you.'

Despite the seriousness of her situation Alice was unable to keep the amusement out of her voice.

'I do not believe what I'm hearing,' she said.

'Have I said something amusing?' Mike demanded, loosening his tie.

'It sounded as though you were sticking up for me.'

'I've never been against you,' Mike insisted.

'You didn't look too put out when I told you Jack and I were history. In fact if my memory serves me correctly you looked relieved. I mean the daughter of a Canadian blue collar worker, whose grandmother lived in a log cabin and shot bears, is hardly going to be a suitable match for a Preston, is she?'

'Don't talk like that.' Mike sounded angry.

'Why not? It's the truth.'

'You don't understand. Jack and I

went through a tough time after our father died. Jack was barely out of his teens. I suppose I've always taken on the role of looking after him. It's a habit I find difficult to break.'

'Are you going to spend the rest of your life making excuses for him?'

A flush worked its way up Mike's neck.

'David Liu,' he said, reverting to a matter of fact voice, 'is one of the festival co-ordinators. If a jade turtle is scheduled to be a part of the exhibition he'll know about it.'

'And if it is, what do I do? Steal it and give it over to Lan? That would definitely have the authorities on my doorstep, wouldn't you say?'

Mike's mobile ringtone interrupted them. Alice leaned back in her seat while he took the call. There were many shortcomings she could lay at Jack's door but she couldn't believe he was a thief.

'I have to be somewhere — five minutes ago,' Mike informed her.

'Well, thanks for trying to help.' Alice retrieved her bag off the seat next to Mike.

'Not so fast.' Rummaging in his pocket Mike produced a small card. 'Check out the orchid display. This invitation will get you in. Go along and see what you can find out. Chat to David and,' he added, 'be careful.'

'Surely you're not expecting trouble at a flower show?'

'I don't know what I'm expecting but where Jack's concerned it's wise to be prepared for anything.'

Alice pocketed the invitation.

'Dinner later?' Mike suggested. 'You can update me on your progress.'

'I'll think about it,' Alice replied.

A welcome slap of rain hit her in the face as she opened the coffee shop door. She stepped out on to the damp pavement. The jade mosaic had been washed away, along with her hope that Mike Preston would do anything positive to help her.

In Search of the Truth

'Alice is a beautiful name. It means the truth, does it not?'

'I believe it does.' Alice nodded.

Although she had only just met him, there was something relaxing in the demeanour of the dignified older man.

'And you are a seeker of the truth.'

A sea of colour had greeted Alice as she had wandered through the stunning collection of orchids. Elegant hostesses clad in silk gowns similar to the one Lan Nguyen had been wearing guided the guests through the dense foliage designed to recreate the natural conditions of the orchids' natural habitat, the lush green of the Tropics.

'Orchids,' their hostess informed them, 'are a thriving industry and make an important contribution to the economy. New species are constantly being discovered, creating a never-ending task for the botanists whose job it is to keep their records up to date. Orchids are no longer the rare plants they once were.'

Eager to look round on her own, Alice had broken away from the main group and while she paused to inspect a flower that resembled a scarlet foxglove she became aware of a bald-headed man of indeterminate age standing patiently by her side. His face was unlined but his complexion bore evidence of many hours spent in the sun. He bowed deeply.

'I do not like to disturb your contemplations, but I think perhaps you are looking for me? My name is too complicated for Western tongues so I call myself David Liu.'

'Alice Fairfax.' She returned his greeting with a courteous bow.

'You are interested in orchids?' David asked.

Alice took a deep breath.

'Actually, I am interested in turtles.'

'Turtles are not my specialist subject,' he said with a regretful smile. 'I have to confess I don't swim so I have never seen them in their natural habitat.'

'Do you know anything about jade turtles?' Alice asked in a careful voice.

David made another slight inclination of his head but did not answer her question.

'May I invite you to share some refreshment with me? I have been on my feet all day and I am sure you deserve a break, too.'

Alice hesitated, not sure if David Liu was being polite or if he really wanted to share a cup of tea with a female who had asked him a question he seemed reluctant to answer.

'Thank you.' Alice decided to accept his offer.

She followed David as he shuffled towards a discreet tent hidden away from public view. She flinched as they passed a reptile display. Snakes unsettled her. Jack had scoffed at her fears, insisting the only way to face up to fears was to challenge them. He'd then draped a python around her neck. The memory of its scales on Alice's flesh was not something she would easily forget.

'Please make yourself comfortable.'

David indicated a large rush mat covered in an array of silk cushions running the length of the far side of the tent. It created a haven of rest of water displays, lemongrass, low lights and gentle background music in the middle of a busy exhibition. Orchid petals floated in bowls of fresh water.

Alice leaned back against one of the cushions and watched David prepare the tea. His unhurried movements suggested he was a man who was at peace with life. He waited for the tea to infuse before pouring it into delicate cups.

'You have, I think, something on your mind.' He joined her on the rush mat. 'If I can help with your quest I am prepared to listen.'

'My quest?' Alice queried in surprise.

'We are all searching for something.'

'I didn't know my intention was that obvious.'

'I have been watching you wander through the plants. You acknowledge their beauty but this is not the reason why you are here.'

'What are you searching for?' Alice asked, intrigued.

'I live in harmony with the universe,' David explained with a roguish smile, his dark brown eyes reflecting his amusement, 'which makes me sound unbearably complacent, does it not?'

'Not at all.' Alice smiled, warming towards him.

'You are beginning to relax. Good. Life will take you where it wants you to go but it is inevitable that we shall make a few wrong turns along the way.'

'You should try life coaching,' Alice insisted.

'I am not a teacher. I like to observe life.'

'And what have you observed about me?'

'Please, I want to be your friend.'
David finished his tea. 'What I have
observed is not important. You need to
know something. I will help if I can. You
mentioned jade turtles?'

Alice was unsure what to make of
this exceptional man sitting on the rush
mat next to her.

'I assume you want to know if they
are valuable?'

'It seems out of place to mention
materialism in such a tranquil environ-
ment.'

'Not at all. I said I would help you in
your quest so please go ahead. Ask your
questions.'

'Do you know Lan Nguyen?'

A mask came over David's face.

'Have I said something to upset you?'

'May I call you Alice?' David asked.

'Of course.

'Words of advice, dear Alice, do not
have more to do with Lan than you
need to.'

'I don't understand.'

'I don't like talking about people

behind their backs but there are things you should know.'

'Go on,' Alice urged.

'Lan claims to be of royal descent.'

'What is she doing in Saltwich?' Alice butted in. 'I mean a college town on the east coast? It's hardly her natural habitat.'

'Patience.' David held up a hand and Alice lapsed into silence.

'Lan's background is far from regal. She lived in a stilted house with her grandparents.'

'A stilted house?' Alice raised her eyebrows.

'They are basic structures and have to be built of wood because the river beneath them floods. At low tide you can use a ladder to gain access. At high tide you need a boat. There is of course nothing wrong with coming from such a humble background but Lan wanted more out of life.

'She changed her name — her real one is now lost in the mists of time — and when the chance came to seek a

40

better life she took it. She was eventually granted sanctuary in France. That is where I first met her. For a while we were friends.

'I worked for a jeweller as a delivery man. Some goods went missing. Naturally I was the chief suspect. I protested my innocence and although I was never officially accused I felt I couldn't stay on in the job.'

'Are you saying Lan is a jewel thief?'

'I know nothing for certain, but instinct told me she was implicated in what happened.'

'What did you do about it?'

'What could I do? I had no proof.'

'And Lan?'

'The next time I heard of her she claimed to be an international business-woman.'

Alice sensed her line of questioning was a part of David's past he wanted to put behind him but with time running out before she had to contact Lan again she needed to know more.

'I was told a jade turtle would

perhaps be on display during the festival?'

David paused.

'You should speak to Netta McKenzie.'

'Who?'

'She and her husband Claud were great friends of my wife and me.'

'You're married?' Alice found it difficult to contain her surprise.

A look of intense sadness flitted across David's face.

'My wife has been laid to rest.'

'I'm sorry.'

'We had many happy years together. I must be grateful for that. After Pearl died I continued to travel the world, sometimes with Netta and her husband, a custom Netta and I have continued now we are both on our own.' The twinkle was back in David's eyes. 'Our relationship is very respectable, I assure you,' he added.

'I'm sure it is,' Alice agreed.

'And I have to confess I do have an ulterior motive in asking you to speak to my dear Netta for me.'

'You do?'

'I apologise. I am getting ahead of myself.' David made a bow. 'Netta's husband Claud Brisson was an expert on Oriental art. He told me a story, more of a fairy tale, really, that an emperor commissioned a magnificent jade turtle, which he intended to offer up in a special ceremony honouring his ancestors.

'Claud believed that the turtle story was a myth, like your Loch Ness Monster, but that doesn't stop greedy individuals wanting to make money out of a fairy tale. The real turtle is always being dug up or rediscovered.'

'And why do I need to speak to your friend Netta?'

'Because she has promised to loan us her jade turtle for the duration of the exhibition, merely as an exhibit, nothing else. It's not real or particularly valuable but it would be of some interest to visitors.'

'What sort of security would you

have in place?' Alice asked. 'I mean in case someone wanted to . . . ' She paused, uncertain how to go on.

'Misappropriate it?'

'Yes.'

'If Lan is thinking of stealing it, tell her,' David evaded another direct answer, 'no dice.'

'Will you introduce me to Netta?' Alice asked.

A small sigh escaped David's lips.

'Netta is being — difficult,' David admitted.

'Over the loan of the turtle?'

'No, over a more a personal matter, now she will not answer my texts. She is stubborn like a mule and if she doesn't want to do something then she won't.'

'What have you asked her to do?'

'I proposed deepening our relationship. Marriage,' David admitted with an embarrassed smile, 'but Netta said she valued her independence too much to even consider the idea.'

It was Alice's turn to feel uncomfortable.

'I don't think I should get involved in your personal life.'

'Marriage proposals aside,' David dismissed her objection with a wave of his hand, 'I can't stop worrying about Netta. On her travels she has camped out in most remote areas of the world and never suffered the slightest illness but the years are catching up with her. She has no family and lives alone but she will not listen to me when I tell her she needs a companion.'

Before Alice could reply, one of the hostesses approached, bowed and waited patiently by David's side.

'I must go. Will you visit Netta? Use the turtle as an excuse.'

'Where does she live?'

'Off the coast road in an old farmhouse.' David's grip on Alice's arm was surprisingly firm. 'Let me know how she is. Please?'

'I'll do my best.'

'Thank you so much.' David beamed at her. 'It was a fortuitous day when fate crossed our mutual paths.'

With her head still in something of a whirl Alice made her way back to her car. Hesitating, she sat in the driving seat for a few moments then, uncertain whether or not she was doing the right thing, she headed out towards the coast road.

Unexpected Invitation

'Netta McKenzie.' Mike frowned. 'I haven't heard that name in a while.'

'Who is she?' Alice demanded.

'Never mind about Netta, where have you been for the past two days?'

'Here and there,' Alice replied evasively.

'You promised to keep in touch.'

'I only said I might.'

'I've been out of my mind with worry.'

'Have you?' It was Alice's turn to sound surprised.

'Has Lan Nguyen contacted you?'

The sight of the deep fried prawns delivered to a neighbouring table made Alice's stomach rumble. She'd only agreed to have dinner with Mike when he appeared outside her studio and threatened to evict her if she didn't come out and talk to him.

The smell of fragrant lemon rice wafting towards her reminded Alice she hadn't eaten properly for days.

She broke a breadstick in two then dropped it on to her side plate. Hungry as she was, her appetite threatened to desert her.

'You're Jack Preston's brother,' she said in a voice devoid of emotion.

'That is not news to me,' Mike clipped back at her.

'How do I know you won't let me down, too?'

'I know your trust in our family has taken a serious knock,' he began, 'but I am trying to put things right, otherwise I wouldn't have come chasing after you, would I?'

'I suppose not,' Alice conceded.

'And as you're still here and in one piece I'm going to assume you've heard nothing further from Lan.'

'No, I haven't.'

'Right then, back to business. You were enquiring after Netta McKenzie.' Mike took up the thread of Alice's earlier enquiry. 'To the best of my knowledge she has been retired for years.

'In her day she went places no respectable female dared venture and reported back on all sorts of atrocities. She won shedloads of awards and bluffed her way out of goodness knows how many dangerous situations. She was in your face before the expression had been invented.'

'I see.'

'How did you hear about her?'

'From David Liu.'

'You went to see him? What did he have to say for himself?'

'He told me that the jade turtle that's going to be on display belongs to Netta.'

'Then we are making progress, aren't we?'

'Not really. According to David, it's not worth stealing.'

'Hmm,' Mike mused, 'this is getting complicated. What's Netta's take on the situation?'

'I didn't get to see her.'

'I thought you said you did.'

'It's another complication,' Alice admitted.

'Try me.'

Alice took a deep breath.

'David asked me to check up on Netta.'

'Why?'

Before Alice could reply, their dishes were delivered to the table.

'Tuck in,' Mike urged. 'We can talk as we go along.'

Alice forked up some steamed jasmine rice then helped herself to a spicy fishcake.

'David is worried because Netta isn't taking his calls.'

'I know the feeling,' Mike muttered, casting Alice a baleful look. 'Sorry, on you go,' he added.

'I drove out to Netta's farmhouse,' Alice continued, 'and knocked on the door. A voice through the letterbox informed me in no uncertain terms that visitors were unwelcome. When I mentioned David Liu's name the flap was firmly snapped back into place. I rang the bell several more times but Netta didn't open the door.'

'How do you know it was Netta?'

'I don't, actually.'

Mike pursed his lips.

'I've heard she can be difficult.'

'That's it, really,' Alice said. 'My deadline with Lan has passed and she hasn't been in touch with me again, so I've more or less decided to call her bluff. If Jack was involved in stealing Netta's turtle then it was nothing to do with me and if Lan wants the return of her advance then she's going to have to wait for Jack to come back off honeymoon and ask him for it.' Alice helped herself to more rice before smiling at Mike.

'Of course, if I do hear from Lan I could put her in touch with you.'

'What do you want to do that for?' Mike asked with a puzzled frown.

'As Jack's next of kin you can explain how it's only a misunderstanding and that your brother is really a good guy at heart and if she won't take your word for it you can come up with the money.'

The moment Alice spoke she feared she may have gone too far.

'You know,' Mike looked hard at her, 'my mother once mentioned you as the sweet little girl who liked eating fruit cake in her garden.'

Alice's face felt unaccountably warm at the memory. Mike's mother had been kind to her and although Alice was tall for her age had never made her feel clumsy or gauche.

'She always said I was special,' Alice admitted, 'even though my father was only a gardener.'

'My mother would have been the last person in the world to think like that,' Mike protested.

Alice, faced with the indignation in Mike's eyes, was forced to look down at the broken breadstick on her plate. Her father would have taken her to task too for making such an insensitive remark. He was a bluff but fair man who had always admired Mrs Preston and the way she treated everyone with courtesy and charm.

Taking a deep breath, Alice raised her eyes to Mike's.

'Do you think we could start again?'

'You mean we should work as a team,' a smile tugged the corner of Mike's mouth, 'to bring down the forces of evil.'

Alice felt a weight lift from her shoulders. Her bond with Jack had started in much the same way but this time she felt they were playing with a different set of rules.

'I'd like that.'

'Then I'm up for it too.' Mike poured some more wine and raised his glass to Alice. 'Here's to us.'

'To us,' Alice returned the toast.

'Out of interest . . . ' Mike paused, 'and you can tell me to mind my own business if you like.'

'Go on,' Alice urged intrigued.

'How did you and Jack get together? Professionally, I mean?'

'On a flight from Toronto to London.'

'What was Jack doing in Canada?'

'I have no idea. He's your brother.'

'That doesn't make me his keeper. I'll try another question. What were you doing in Canada?'

'I was visiting my father.'

'It's been years since I've seen him. How is he?'

'Robust as ever.'

'I seem to remember he didn't suffer fools gladly and he wasn't above taking my mother to task if he thought her suggestions for the garden were over the top. 'Too cultivated' was how he once put it.'

'He went organic long before it became so fashionable.'

'And he's settled back in Canada now?'

'He remarried after my mother died. I had been staying with him and his new wife after I was made redundant. I was a hotel receptionist but it closed down.'

'You have had a run of bad luck,' Mike sympathised.

Alice knew it was important to remember that Mike's brother was the cause of all her problems and that it wouldn't do to completely lower her guard.

'Do you like graphic designing?' She changed the subject.

'I like giving brands a visual presence, but as with all jobs it has its ups and downs.'

'You didn't follow your father into the army?'

Mike repressed a shudder.

'Neither Jack nor I wanted to go down that route.'

'Why not?'

'Families, you know,' Mike glossed over his answer. 'Will you be going back to Canada when all this is over?' he asked.

'I can't. My father and stepmother delayed their deep-sea diving honeymoon because of me. Kaye comes from Perth and they may settle in Australia.'

Alice paused, surprised to realise that Mike was actually listening to her. Jack had been more interested in the sound of his own voice.

'You're welcome to stay on at the studio for as long as you like. I have to confess I was guilty of overstepping my authority when I threatened to evict you. It's not within my power to do such a thing.'

'I thought it belonged to your family trust.'

'It belongs to Jack.'

Alice blinked.

'Then he won't want me staying on, will he?'

'I'm sure Jack has other things on his mind at the moment.'

'What about you?'

'Me?'

'Don't you want the studio?'

'Why would I?'

'I don't know. For your design work?'

'I have my own flat and my own studio and before you start on again about the privileged Prestons,' Mike cautioned, 'I paid for them out of my own pocket.'

'Thank you,' Alice said in a quiet voice.

'What for?' Mike cast her another suspicious glance.

'For letting me stay on in the studio.'

An expression Alice didn't understand crossed Mike's face.

'To get back to the matter in hand,' he sipped some wine, 'I suspect Jack left his affairs in a mess.'

'Lan isn't our only dissatisfied client,' Alice admitted, 'although she is being the most awkward.'

'If she should appear again then we'd best make sure we have something to tell her.' Mike put out a hand to steady Alice's as her emotions threatened to get the better of her.

'It's not your problem,' she insisted.

'Neither was it entirely Jack's fault,' Mike replied.

'So you're still saying it's mine?' Alice snatched her hand away from Mike's.

'Stop being so spiky. All I'm trying to

say is that after Jack's allowance dried up he carried on as though nothing had happened.'

'His allowance dried up?'

Mike shook his head.

'There are funds I am sure my mother intended for Jack and myself but my father in his wisdom thought otherwise. I think Jack was trying to make a go of things, only he seems to have failed spectacularly and you don't knock a man when he's down, especially not when he's your brother.'

'Jack seems to have looked after himself well enough. He went off, married an heiress and left you to pick up the pieces.'

'I'm sure it will come right in the end.'

'I wish I shared your optimism.'

'Things could be worse.'

'I fail to see how.'

'Jack could have married you.' A wry smile curved Mike's lips. 'Then you really would have something to be spiky about.'

The heat from the hot plate on the table made Alice feel uncomfortably warm.

'Have you had any luck tracing what happened to Lan's advance?' Mike's question filled the silence that had fallen between them.

'None at all. All I know is from what David Liu said any supposedly accredited turtles on display have to be fakes. Lan must be aware of this so why would she want Jack to steal a fake?'

'No idea, but I have found out something. I would have told you earlier but I couldn't get hold of you.'

The flush on Alice's face deepened.

'Go on,' she mumbled through a mouthful of sweet and sour sauce.

Mike waved a chopstick at the last spring roll.

'Go halves?'

'It's yours. I want to leave room for dessert.'

'I'm glad you've regained your appetite. It's brought colour to your cheeks.'

'Research,' Alice prompted, wishing Mike's eyes weren't such a deep blue. Jack's were the same and she had learned to her cost that it was a colour not to be trusted.

'Selling bogus turtles is a lucrative business. Validation certificates are easily faked but it's difficult to keep up a good supply of authentic-looking turtles. It's a dying skill, apparently, so the first showing of Netta's turtle is bound to create a lot of interest. My thinking is what if Lan has a buyer lined up but needs a turtle?'

Alice gaped at him.

'You're not serious.'

'And she had lined up Jack to be her fall guy if anything went wrong.'

'No.' Alice shook her head. 'Any buyer of repute would know the market is flooded with fakes.'

'There are some people who believe the Loch Ness Monster really exists.'

'David Liu said much the same thing — about the myth being good for business.'

'Exactly.'

Mike signalled for the dessert menu.

'How about mango and sticky coconut rice?' Mike ordered then turned back to face Alice. 'I have another suggestion,' he said.

'You don't have to get involved,' Alice insisted, feeling the situation was slipping out of her control.

'You're right, I don't, but you need to start the healing process and you can't do that until Jack is out of the picture.'

'I'm already over Jack so there's no need to play nursemaid.'

'No, you're not over Jack.'

Robbed of breath by Mike's arrogance Alice pushed back her chair.

'That is an outrageous remark.'

'You're too prickly by half to convince me you haven't got him out of your system and where do you think you're going? Sticky coconut rice?' he coaxed.

'I don't want any dessert.'

'And how about going to the yellow party later?'

The waiter delivered their desserts to the table.

'The yellow party?' she repeated.

'Yellow symbolises good fortune and the festival officially kicks off tonight with a yellow party for which I have been given a ticket. Will you be my plus one?'

Mike picked up his spoon. Alice wavered then sat down again.

'Tell me more,' she said, following his example.

'The rule is guests have to wear something yellow. I've got a psychedelic tie hidden away in a drawer, I bought it when I was going through an alternative phase. What about you?'

'Would a sunhat do?' Alice spoke without thinking before she realised her question had signified assent.

'Perfect.' Mike plunged his spoon into his sticky rice. 'Eat up, then we'll be on our way.'

★   ★   ★

Mike linked his arm through Alice's.

'Hold on tight, things look like they could get rowdy.'

The area adjacent to the Tao centre was a sea of yellow, thronged with party-goers intent on having a good time. On stage, musicians decked out in gold sequinned waistcoats were doing a magnificent job of whipping up the atmosphere. People of all generations were dancing and swaying along to the music.

'There's David,' Alice pointed to a dignified figure dressed in dusky yellow silk gliding towards them, his face wreathed in smiles.

'I am so pleased you have come.' He pressed his hands together and bowed to Alice. 'Welcome to our yellow party and may your life be prosperous in every way.'

'Thank you.' Alice inclined her head.

'What a beautiful hat. The sunflowers are magnificent.'

'As is the embroidery on your jacket,' Alice said, admiring the intricate needlework.

'My wife was an accomplished needlewoman.'

'No-one's complimented me on my tie.' Mike undid his jacket and proudly revealed a loosely knotted tangerine affair draped around his neck.

'You have indeed made a great effort.' David's eyes crinkled with amusement.

Mike looked suspiciously from David to Alice.

'What?'

'Mike,' Alice said, 'it's terrible.'

Mike gave it a tweak.

'It's yellow — sort of.'

'That is all that matters.' David indicated the lantern lit path that stretched down to the marquee. 'Pass, friends, and have a good evening.'

'Will Netta be here?' Alice asked.

'Unfortunately she is still not taking my calls,' David looked disappointed. 'If you will excuse me I have to attend to my other guests. There are refreshments available and a variety of entertainments. Enjoy.'

'What's going on with David and Netta?' Mike asked as David bustled off.

'He asked her to marry him and she turned him down.'

'Good for Netta.'

'You don't approve of marriage?' Alice took a step backwards in surprise.

'I'm all for it — unless it's between you and Jack.'

'Let's not go there,' Alice warned.

'He was wrong for you, Alice. That's why I made such a fuss about your relationship.'

'We agreed tonight would be Jack free,' Alice insisted.

'I don't remember agreeing to anything of the kind.'

'We are here to work. It was you who said if Lan should come back into my life we should have something ready for her.'

'I actually said our lives but let's not split hairs. Things look quieter over there.' Mike indicated some empty chairs lined up outside the marquee.

'Why don't we sit down and hatch a plan?'

The sun was washing the sky a gentle pink and turning the tips of the grass orange before it slipped behind a distant clump of trees.

'Look out.' Mike ducked as a group of exuberant party-goers scattered them with stardust. He winced as Alice dug her fingernails into his arm. 'Hey, watch what you're doing.'

'Over there,' Alice pointed.

Mike turned his attention in the direction of the stage.

'What am I looking at?'

'Lan Nguyen.'

'Are you sure?'

'I'd know that hairdo anywhere.'

'Who's the man she's talking to?'

'Come on.' Alice dragged Mike to his feet. 'This could be the lead we're looking for.' She broke into a brisk trot. 'Hurry up, we don't want to lose sight of them.'

Sprinting over the stardust-flecked grass Alice didn't bother to see if Mike was following her. She had to know what Lan was up to and who she was with.

As she got nearer the stage a toga-clad dancer grabbed her arm, twirled her round and began an energetic routine. His partner grabbed Mike by the arm and proved equally impossible to shake off.

Alice wriggled free as swiftly as she could and ducked under the rope encircling the slightly more dignified atmosphere of the VIP lounge.

'May I help you, madam?' A hostess shimmered towards her.

Alice flashed her best smile.

'I thought I saw a friend of mine come in here.'

'This area is by invitation only.'

'Mr Preston?' She traded his name with what she hoped was a winning smile.

'The name is not on my list, madam.'

'You must have heard of him. He's the chief graphic designer.'

The unperturbed official bowed.

'I'll show you to the exit, madam. It's this way.'

Alice cast a frantic look around the lounge.

'That gentleman there,' she pointed towards a guest who was engrossed in reading a sheet of paper he held in his hands. 'Do you know his name?'

'That's Selwyn Bishop,' a voice behind them interrupted. Alice swung round to face a woman dressed in an outrageous kimono decorated with fire breathing dragons, 'and unless I am very much mistaken, you are the young woman who was hammering on my door the other day. The name is Netta McKenzie.'

A Thief in Their Midst

'Come and sit down over here.' Netta waved the attendant away. 'This young lady is my guest. I'll vouch for her.'

'Does David Liu know you are here?' Alice cast a furtive look over her shoulder.

'Who?' Netta enquired with studied indifference.

'Your friend David,' Alice insisted.

'I don't know and I don't care. Do you know he had the nerve to propose marriage? I mean, at my age? I told him in no uncertain terms that the answer was no.'

'He is worried about you. He told me you haven't been well and that you live alone.'

'Ha.' Netta settled down into a rattan chair and with a regal gesture indicated that Alice was to sit beside her. 'So apart from wondering about the state of my health why were you hammering on my door?'

'It's a long story,' Alice hesitated.

'Does it involve a man?'

'Sort of.'

'I thought so. What's your connection with Selwyn Bishop?'

'I don't have one.'

'Then why are you interested in him?'

'He was talking to Lan Nguyen.'

From the look Netta cast in her direction Alice suspected she had scored another black mark against this formidable lady.

'Talking of men there's one over there trying to attract your attention.'

Alice swung round to see an agitated Mike gesturing in her direction.

'Is he with you?'

'Yes,' she admitted.

Netta beckoned to a female attendant.

'Ask that young man to join us, please.' She used a tone of voice Alice was beginning to recognise. It dared anyone to argue with her. The attendant did as she was bid.

'Someone,' Netta turned her attention back to Alice, 'is going to have to take him in hand fashion wise. That tie is atrocious.'

A smile played on Alice's lips. Despite her stubborn character she liked Netta.

'It's a yellow party, isn't it — yin and yang?'

'There's yellow and yellow.' Netta's greeny grey eyes softened. 'You know, your friend reminds me of my beloved Claud. He was the only man I ever listened to. You'd do well to listen to this one. He has the same way about him.'

Alice opened her mouth to object but was immediately hushed by Netta.

'Here he comes.'

Mike crossed the grass towards them.

'I don't think we should be here, Alice,' he cautioned, 'it's for invited guests only.'

'And you are my invited guests.

Name?' Netta barked at him.

'Mike Preston, Miss McKenzie,' Mike stuttered, taken aback.

'Netta will do. What's going on here?' she demanded.

'It's all been a bit of a misunderstanding,' Mike tried to explain.

'Sit down next to your friend.' She indicated Alice. 'By the way, young woman, you didn't tell me your name.'

'Alice Fairfax.'

'Hmm.' Netta turned to Mike. 'She's independent, like me.'

Mike, raising his eyes at Alice, gestured towards the exit.

'Preston?' Netta frowned. 'Are you by any chance related to Jack Preston?'

'He's my brother.'

'He's another one who turned up on my doorstep and shouted through my letterbox.'

'Was his visit anything to do with your turtle?' Alice leaned forward.

'I don't know, I didn't answer.'

'And?' Alice coaxed when Netta lapsed into silence.

'I never heard from him again,' was Netta's reply. 'He didn't strike me as a stayer.' She sniffed and peered at Mike. 'And you say he's your brother?'

'Yes.'

'He's better looking than you.' She turned to Alice. 'What's your connection with this Jack?'

'He and I were business partners,' Alice admitted.

'Were you, indeed?'

'He accepted a commission from Lan Nguyen regarding your turtle.' Alice hesitated, reluctant to go into further details.

'Then why isn't he here?' Netta asked. 'It's on full display. I brought it over this evening.'

'Because he's on his honeymoon,' Mike interrupted.

Netta's eyes narrowed.

'And what happened about this so-called commission?'

'I'm trying to sort things out,' Alice admitted, 'but it's proving difficult.'

'Why don't you tell Lan the deal's off?'

'Because we can't find out what my brother has done with the advance she gave him,' Mike said.

'Tricky,' Netta agreed, her eyes darting to and fro as she looked round the assembled throng. 'Alice tells me you want to know what Lan Nguyen was doing talking to Selwyn Bishop?'

Alice wished Netta would keep her voice down. People were beginning to look in their direction.

'Yes,' Mike replied.

'Why?'

'It's difficult to know where to start,' Alice admitted.

'Good,' Netta broke into a smile, 'I like it when things aren't straightforward. It arouses my journalistic instinct. Conflict always makes better copy.'

'It also makes it more difficult to put into words,' Alice said.

'Have some candy while you think about it.' Netta passed a paper bag around. 'Tell you what, why don't I go first and tell you what I know about Lan Nguyen?'

'I'm good with that,' Mike replied.

'Is Lan from round here?' Alice asked.

'With those looks?' Netta raised an eyebrow. 'To be honest I'm not sure exactly what part of the world she comes from. Sometimes she gives out the story that she's a princess who's down on her luck, but if you believe that you'd believe anything. I've bumped into her several times on my travels. Claud mistrusted her and that was enough for me.'

'David mentioned she lived in a stilted house, somewhere on the Indochina peninsula. They are wooden constructions,' Alice explained.

'I know what they are,' Netta interrupted. 'I've even stayed in one on my travels. There isn't a part of the world I haven't visited at one time or another. I was a war correspondent, you know, in the days before females did that sort of thing.

My father didn't approve. He wanted me to take a secretarial course but I would have died in an office. I did do the shorthand and typing course but that's as far as it went. Where was I?' Netta ground to a halt.

'You were going to tell us about Selwyn Bishop,' Mike reminded her.

'Have you finished with those?'

Netta snatched back her bag of sweets and rammed it into the voluminous bag she was clutching.

'I don't know what part of the world Selwyn comes from either. He speaks with an American accent but I think he acquired that on his travels. I also suspect Selwyn Bishop is not his real name. That's something else he acquired along the way. He calls himself an international entrepreneur who likes collecting things.'

'What sort of things?' Alice asked.

'Oriental art.'

'Is that his connection to Lan Nguyen?'

'I couldn't say, but he has tried to

buy my jade turtle from me on more than one occasion.'

'David suggested it was a present from your husband,' Alice spoke carefully, hoping the mention of David's name wouldn't send Netta off on another of her tirades against him.

'It was.' Netta spoke in a softer voice and looked down at her colourful plaid bag. 'He gave it to me on our tenth wedding anniversary.'

Mike cast Alice a puzzled look but before either of them could speak there was a disturbance in a far corner of the tent.

'What's happening now?' Netta demanded.

Selwyn Bishop thrust the sheet of paper he had been studying into his pocket and cast a furtive look in their direction as if he suspected they had been talking about him.

'I have no idea,' Mike replied.

Netta's face lit up.

'I nearly didn't come this evening.

Parties aren't really my scene any more but things are looking up.'

'It's gone.' An agitated David Liu hurried through the tent flap as fast as his dignity would allow.

'What's gone?' Netta demanded.

'It was there earlier this evening — the turtle,' he emphasised as a sea of puzzled faces turned in his direction.

'You mean you've lost it already?' Netta demanded.

'Ms Nguyen and I were only admiring it a few moments ago.' Selwyn spoke in a deep assured voice.

'Then you are probably responsible for its disappearance,' Netta accused him.

'I beg your pardon?' Selwyn turned towards her.

'You've been after it for ages.'

'This was nothing to do with me,' Selwyn insisted. 'I have been sitting here studying paperwork for at least ten minutes and there are numerous witnesses to testify to that fact, yourself and your companions included.'

'Careful what you say, Netta,' Mike cautioned.

'Netta?' David paled. 'I didn't know you were here.'

'Now I am you can tell me exactly what happened.'

David's face was screwed up in anguish.

'The light was on in the exhibition room,' he explained. 'I went to turn it off and I found the cabinet had been broken into and the turtle was missing. It can only have been gone a few minutes.'

'Then I suggest a full body search of everyone present.'

'You can't do that. Have you never heard of human rights?' Selwyn demanded.

'I've heard a lot of things, Mr Bishop, especially about you.'

'Before we get too personal,' Mike said loudly, 'might it be an idea to contact the police?'

'I'm not having them involved.' Netta

dismissed the suggestion with a wave of her hand.

'You mean you don't want to press charges?' Alice could not keep the surprise out of her voice.

'I do not.'

'But the turtle means so much to you.'

'Exactly — it's my turtle and I make the rules. Now, I have a new commission for you, Alice Fairfax. You find my turtle and I'll pay Lan whatever it is you owe her and I'll pay you a retainer.'

'Miss McKenzie — Netta,' Mike implored.

'You can help her, if you like. Come and see me tomorrow. No, thank you, David, I do not require a lift home. My driver is outside. This has proved a far more exciting evening than I could have imagined. Quite like old times. Good night, everyone.'

Netta's exit was followed by silence.

Sealed With a Kiss

'What are we going to do?' Alice demanded.

'Exactly as Netta suggests.' David's soft voice provided a welcome contrast to the confusion erupting around them. 'She always gets her own way in the end. Experience has taught me it is easier to give in.' His eyes twinkled in admiration. 'Isn't she magnificent?'

'Not the word I'd use.' Mike appeared not to share David's enthusiasm. 'Selwyn Bishop is still glaring at us and I can't say I blame him.'

'Netta does take some getting used to,' David agreed. 'I have known her for many years and I still don't completely understand what makes her tick.'

'Let's hope Selwyn Bishop doesn't take her accusations further,' Mike said.

'Then to stop him we have to find the turtle,' Alice said.

'David, didn't you have any security keeping an eye on the exhibits?' Mike asked.

'We have twenty-four hour camera surveillance — of a sort.' David's expression did not fill Alice with confidence.

'What do you mean?' Mike demanded.

'The machine,' David chose his words carefully, 'is old and I think second hand. I'm not even sure if it was operating tonight. My fault,' he admitted. 'I have never really seen the need to alarm personal possessions. It goes against my beliefs. Do you wish to see the scene of the crime?' he asked Alice and Mike.

'Why is it whenever Jack gets involved in anything it always goes pear-shaped?' Mike ran an exasperated hand through his hair.

'Who is Jack?' David asked.

'My brother,' Mike replied.

'And my business partner,' Alice bit her lip. 'He accepted a commission from Lan.'

'To steal the turtle?'

Alice gaped at David in surprise.

'How did you know?'

'Why else would you be interested in its provenance? You are not a collector but Selwyn Bishop is and he is here. Lan Nguyen has been seen talking to him. It cannot be a coincidence. Something is going on.' David paused.

'We don't know that Jack was going to take the turtle,' Alice insisted.

'If that was his intention do you think your brother Jack was maybe successful in his endeavours?' David asked Mike.

'He is in the Caribbean,' Mike replied, 'so I should think it is highly unlikely.'

'What you say is the truth,' David acknowledged.

'We're wasting time,' Alice said. 'The thief could still be on the premises.'

'Perhaps we had better take a look at the crime scene,' Mike suggested, 'then we can decide what to do.'

'Mr Liu?' One of the attendants approached. 'What shall we do with the guests? Some of them have expressed a wish to leave.'

'Persuade them to stay,' David replied. 'Provide more snacks and refreshments and bring the firework display forward. It's a beautiful evening and we don't want it spoiled by a minor inconvenience.'

'It's more than an inconvenience,' Alice murmured to Mike. 'The fallout could be disastrous.'

'Come on,' Mike urged, 'we don't want David getting away.'

Alice hastened after him. The janitor was positioned outside the Tao centre.

'Dawson? I thought you went off duty an hour ago.' David was clearly agitated.

'My wife wanted to stay on for the fireworks.'

'All this evening's events have been most irregular.'

'Did you see anything?' Mike asked the janitor.

'Nothing out of the ordinary, sir. There was a disturbance involving some of the youngsters throwing stardust. Things were getting out of hand. I was called over to calm everyone down. I got back to my post just as the theft was discovered. It was nothing to do with me,' he said, as if expecting to be blamed for the incident.

'No-one's saying it was,' David soothed him. 'Miss Fairfax and Mr Preston are here to inspect the damage.'

'Anything you say, sir.'

Dawson stepped to one side.

'Could Lan Nguyen be involved?' Alice asked Mike as they followed David inside.

'If Selwyn Bishop has been getting impatient and demanding results, anything's possible I suppose, but I would have thought breaking and entering was hardly her style.'

'Take care with your feet,' David pointed to the shards of glass littering the floor.

Alice inspected the empty display case. All that remained was a plinth and a description of Netta's jade turtle.

'Mr Liu said he wasn't sure if Miss McKenzie was going to release the turtle for public display and I've been rushed off my feet all day. I can't do everything.'

'So anyone could have taken the turtle?'

The janitor looked down at the ground, unable to face the scorn on Alice's face.

'Wasn't my fault,' he mumbled.

'It was my fault,' David attempted to pacify him.

'So your janitor keeps telling us.' Alice was finding it difficult to hide her dislike of the man. 'Didn't you see anything suspicious?' she persisted.

'No.'

'Did anyone linger longer than usual?'

'There were so many people coming and going I don't think I would have noticed.' The stubborn look was back on Dawson's face.

'Who discovered the turtle was missing?'

'I was closing up for the evening,'

David explained. 'I did my rounds to make sure all the visitors had left. When I returned the display case was as you see it now.'

'Then whoever took it must still be on the premises,' Alice insisted.

'There are many entrances and exits,' David pointed out.

'Shattering glass makes a noise. Didn't either of you hear anything?' Mike asked.

'The youngsters were noisy, too, sir,' Dawson pointed out, 'and what with the party next door, it wouldn't have been too difficult for someone to choose the right moment to strike.'

'Was the turtle insured?' Mike asked.

'Miss McKenzie would be the one to answer that question, sir,' Dawson replied.

'Not that I know much about these things,' David mused, 'but I think it would be impossible to put a material price on such an unusual artefact.'

'But we all know it was a fake,' Alice pointed out.

'Even fakes have their value,' Mike replied. 'A curiosity price if nothing else.'

'What do you suggest we do now?' Alice asked Mike.

'And what are you going to do about the exhibition, David?' Mike asked him.

'Human nature being what it is,' David replied with quiet certainty, 'word of the theft will get round. Visitors will want to view the site and see the scene of the crime for themselves.'

'An empty display case?' Alice repeated in disbelief.

'You would be surprised, my dear friend,' David replied.

'I suppose you didn't steal it,' Alice felt emboldened to ask, 'as some sort of publicity drive?'

'You are beginning to sound like Netta.' David smiled. 'It is a good idea,' he admitted, 'and there's no doubt it will increase visitor numbers.'

'Sorry,' Alice apologised, ashamed of her accusation, 'of course you didn't take it. Netta would never speak to you again.'

'I do not think she is speaking to me now,' David observed.

'It has to have been an inside job.' Mike was still inspecting the display case.

'Not necessarily,' Dawson intervened.

'What makes you say that?'

'Everyone knew of the possibility of it being on display tonight.'

'Then why didn't you secure the cabinet?' Alice demanded.

'I've already explained I was too busy,' was the janitor's truculent reply.

'Let him finish,' Mike intervened.

'This is a public area. Anyone could have walked in on the slightest pretext.'

'Tonight was invitation only,' Alice said.

'And you acquired an invitation,' Dawson pointed out.

'I came as Mr Preston's guest,' Alice's voice rang round the deserted centre.

'All invitees could bring a guest,' Mike said.

'That's what I'm saying,' Dawson

butted in, 'it was virtually open house.'

'Why don't you go and file an incident report?' David suggested. 'Then you can join your wife for the firework display.'

'If you're sure there's nothing more I can do here.' A relieved Dawson hurried away.

'I think we've also seen everything there is to see,' Mike agreed.

'In that case I will try to set the alarm, although there seems little point in doing so now. You will visit Netta?' David asked. 'She is putting on a brave face but I know the turtle meant a lot to her.'

'I'll go and see her in the morning. I have to know if she meant what she said about retaining my services to help find the turtle,' Alice said.

'It might be better if you both went up to the farmhouse,' David suggested.

'Why?' Alice asked.

'Netta can be difficult if she isn't in the mood for visitors.'

'Then why should it make any

difference who's at the front door?'

'For all her feminist principles Netta is old-fashioned,' David explained, a smile tugging the corner of his mouth. 'She responds well to a male influence.'

'It didn't seem to work with Jack. She didn't open the door to him.'

'I'm still coming with you,' Mike insisted.

Before Alice could object, the sky exploded into a kaleidoscope of green and gold stars.

'The attendants have started the firework display early — a good diversion tactic,' David said, his face lighting up as a magenta rocket whooshed into the air. 'Let me know your decision before you leave, please?'

'Come on.' Mike steered Alice towards the marquee.

'Where are we going?'

'I could do with some refreshment.'

'We've already had dinner.'

'It seems a pity to let the left-over nibbles go to waste. While that lot are looking at the sky I suggest we help ourselves.'

'Don't you see that's how it was done?' Alice grabbed Mike's arm.

Mike inspected the abandoned buffet. 'How what was done?'

'The theft,' Alice nearly knocked the proffered plate out of his hand.

'Saffron rice and chicken in a curry sauce do you?' Mike held up a serving spoon.

'What was everyone looking at when the theft took place?'

Mike plonked a serving on to Alice's plate.

'Why don't you tell me?'

'David had ushered the visitors out of the exhibition and was closing up. The janitor's attention was diverted by the gold dust disturbance. Netta was holding forth in the marquee. Everyone was looking at Netta.'

Mike frowned.

'Get a grip, Alice. She would hardly provide a diversion that allowed some-one to steal her own turtle.'

'No, but it provided a perfect opportunity for the thieves to seize their chance and,' Alice's voice rose in excitement, 'Selwyn Bishop.'

'We're not into accusing him again, are we?'

'What was he studying on his sheet of paper?'

'It could have been anything.'

'Whatever it was he was quick enough to hide it when David broke the news.'

'Because we don't like the look of Selwyn that doesn't make him a criminal and he was in sight the whole time so he has a rock solid alibi, as does Netta and you and me, so the four of us are in the clear.'

'Lan Nguyen doesn't have an alibi and where is she?' Alice asked.

'If she's got any sense she's made off, with or without the turtle.'

'I don't want you getting involved, Mike,' Alice said, coming to an instant decision.

'Too late, you heard David. He

practically ordered me up to Netta's farmhouse.'

'We don't have to do what David says.'

Mike put down his plate and placed his hands on her shoulders.

'Don't you understand I'm trying to make things up to you? The Preston family hasn't exactly treated you well in the past.'

'I don't need you to fight my battles.' Alice longed to wriggle out of Mike's grasp.

'I don't know what Jack was thinking of,' Mike continued, 'but I can't help feeling there's more to this than meets the eye and that we're misjudging him.'

'Then the easiest thing in the world would be for you to contact Viv's father and demand to be put through to your brother on his luxury yacht. Then he can give you his side of the story, can't he?'

'Before I do that I want to be sure of my facts. We're a team, Alice. We have to work together otherwise we'll never find out exactly what happened.'

Mike was standing so close to Alice she could see gold dust sparkling on his eyelashes. Acting on impulse and before she could rethink her decision Alice gave a brief nod. A lopsided smile spread across Mike's face causing Alice's pulse to perform a quick wobble.

'That wasn't too difficult was it?' Before she could react his lips grazed her cheek. 'There, sealed with a kiss.'

Surprise Encounter

Coarse grass scraped the chassis of Alice's car as she bumped down the cart track that led to Netta's farmhouse. Steeling herself for a challenging encounter she had tried ringing Lan's personal number but her calls were continuously directed to voicemail. Selwyn Bishop too had disappeared after the firework display. Even Mike had deserted her.

'I can't get out of it,' he had explained during his earlier brief telephone call when he informed her of an unscheduled visit from the family accountant. 'I think it might have been something Jack arranged in my absence.' He paused. 'I do need to talk to her regarding Jack's . . . changed personal circumstances. I don't know how long I'll be.'

'I can manage Netta on my own,'

Alice assured him.

'Do you want to wait until we're finished? I'm sure the meeting won't take all day.'

'I have to see Netta this morning in case she changes her mind about her offer.'

'Well, don't stand any nonsense from her.'

'I only hope she answers her door.'

'Coming,' Mike replied to a muffled female voice in the background. 'I've got to go. Venetia's arrived. Call me the moment you're free.'

Alice frowned, wondering why she should feel so disturbed that Mike's accountant was female. With a lurch she negotiated a pothole and forced herself to concentrate on the task in hand.

A dented Deux Chevaux sporting French number plates was parked outside the farmhouse. Wondering who the visitor could be, Alice grabbed up the notes she had hurriedly assembled before leaving the studio and strode towards the front door. It was flung open before she could raise the knocker.

A rail-thin female sporting an urchin haircut of green spikes tipped vivid orange stood in the doorway. She was wearing a tight fitting white shirt and jeans sporting a rhinestone bejewelled designer logo on the pocket. Alice nearly lost her footing on the doorstep as she hopped back in surprise.

'Netta,' the female pouted as if continuing an earlier conversation, 'has been driving me mad.' She raised her hands in a gesture of frustration. 'I can get no sense out of her. What is all this about her turtle being stolen?' The feline eyes narrowed. 'Are you responsible? Have you come to return it?'

'What? No!' Alice took another hasty step backwards. 'I haven't got it. I never had it.'

'Then what are you doing here?'

Pulling herself together, Alice straightened up.

'Netta invited me,' she announced in a firm voice.

'When?'

'Last night.'

'How do I know who you are? Netta tells me she has recently been receiving unwanted visits.'

'Look,' Alice's patience was wearing thin, 'where is Netta?'

'Asleep. We sat up until the small hours talking. Me, I do not need much sleep but Netta,' the girl shrugged, 'she is old. She sleeps. She won't be down for hours.' She held the door open wide. 'Come in.'

'Who are you?' Alice demanded, taken aback by the suddenness of the invitation.

'I am Christine Fayette,' she announced, as if expecting Alice to have heard of her. 'Do you like French coffee? I cannot drink the stuff Netta has so I always bring my own. Come in.' The aroma of freshly brewed coffee wafted towards Alice. 'The croissants are a day old so I have warmed them up again.'

The kitchen was a surprisingly cosy room. The morning sun cast patterns on the yellow and white checked tablecloth laid out for breakfast for two.

'I was expecting Netta,' Christine explained, 'but as she is still asleep you will join me.' She turned her back on Alice as she adjusted the coffee machine. 'You know my name but I do not know yours.'

'Alice Fairfax.'

Christine turned round and held out a hand.

'Sit, please. I have prepared our petit déjeuner.'

Despite her slim figure Christine devoured three croissants coated in rich cherry jam and drank several cups of coffee before leaning back with a satisfied expression on her face.

'I am sorry I was so suspicious of you at first,' she said, 'but I'm sure Netta said something about a gentleman visitor making a call today. I do not understand why you are here.'

'Mike Preston has been unavoidably detained,' Alice explained, slightly annoyed that Netta hadn't thought to mention her name to Christine.

'That is a pity. Men liven things up, wouldn't you agree?'

Alice bit her lip. Jack had certainly livened things up.

'I am not sure I do,' she said in a cool voice.

'I know it is not correct to say such things these days but,' she shrugged, 'I am French. I like men.'

'What is your relationship to Netta?' Alice asked, changing the subject.

'I am her granddaughter.'

Alice coughed as she hastily swallowed the last of her coffee.

'David Liu said she had no family.'

'This David is her lover — no?'

Alice felt herself blushing.

'I wouldn't go as far as to say that.'

'Netta tells me he has proposed to her.'

'I believe he has.'

'Then they are in love. It can happen

at any time in your life. I need to check him out. Do you have a lover, Alice?'

'Look, can we get down to business?'

There was something about Christine Fayette that made Alice feel uncomfortable.

'It is this Mike Preston perhaps? You are blushing,' Christine crowed, 'I cannot wait to meet him. He will be joining us later?'

'I don't know,' Alice said in a firm voice. 'Can we please talk about turtles?'

'Actually I am only Netta's — how do you say — step granddaughter?'

Alice stifled her irritation. Christine moved at her own pace and it looked as though Alice was going to have to be patient until they got round to the reason for her visit.

'Really?' She did her best to affect interest.

'Netta was Claud's second wife. Claud was my grandfather. The marriage did not last and they both went off and married other people, but

102

Claud was a good grandfather. When my mother, his daughter, died, he invited me to live with them, but they were always travelling around the world so I stayed in France with my father.'

'I see.'

'I have been working as a representative for a make-up company for several years and I visit Netta whenever I can. As she has no other relatives I like to keep an eye on her. I was worried when I arrived last night and no-one was here, but then Netta returned. I could see she was agitated. When I asked her what was wrong she told me a garbled story about the missing turtle.'

Alice took a deep breath, uncertain how much of the events of the previous evening she should reveal.

'The turtle was on display at the Tao centre.'

'And someone stole it?'

'It disappeared,' Alice agreed.

'And you didn't take it?'

'Certainly not. Wherever did you get that idea?'

'Netta said something about someone disappearing with some money,' Christine sounded vague. 'They were paid to steal it, perhaps?'

'It wasn't quite like that.'

'Was it your Mike Preston?'

'No.'

'Then who was it?'

'My partner was Jack Preston.' Alice hesitated, not sure how to continue.

'They are related?'

'They are brothers.'

'Things begin to make sense.' Christine's smile turned edgy, sending a shiver down Alice's spine. 'You were partners with Jack Preston?'

'Professional and personal,' Alice added before Christine asked the inevitable question.

A satisfied smile spread across Christine's face.

'And how did Jack's brother become involved in your scam?'

'It's not a scam.'

Christine ignored Alice's protest.

'Was he another partner in your little business? What did you do exactly — apart from stealing valuable artefacts?'

Alice wasn't sure it had been a wise move confiding in Christine Fayette on such a short acquaintance. She was too quick to jump to conclusions.

'We didn't steal anything,' she insisted.

'So you say.' Christine looked unconvinced.

'We house sat for people. We collected their parcels if they were away, carried out general domestic duties, that sort of thing.'

'What a boring life,' Christine remarked. 'Stealing turtles, now that sounds much more fun.'

'I wouldn't know.' Alice glanced at her watch, wondering how much longer it would be before Netta put in an appearance.

'Tell me about your relationship with Mike,' Christine invited.

'When I needed to contact Jack I thought perhaps Mike might know where he is.'

'And does he?'

'Yes. Jack Preston is on his honeymoon.'

Christine's blue eyes widened.

'I always thought the English were cold with their emotions. This Jack has fire in his veins.'

'That's one way of putting it.'

'And he deserted you?'

'I suppose he did,' Alice admitted.

'I would not have let any man treat me like that,' she announced. 'You must take revenge.'

'I don't want revenge. I want to talk to him but I can't get hold of him. Jack is on a Caribbean cruise paid for by his father-in-law.'

'And his father-in-law would not want an ex lover anywhere near his daughter's new husband?' Christine's eyes sparkled with intrigue. 'That I understand.' Alice wasn't sure she liked being referred to as an ex-lover.

'Has Netta ever spoken to you about a man called Selwyn Bishop?' Alice asked.

'She may have mentioned his name but it does not, how do you say, ring any bells?'

'He may be interested in buying Netta's turtle.'

'So are many people, but so far she has refused to part with it.'

'Last night she asked me to discover what has happened to it. That's why I'm here.'

Christine frowned and for the first time looked unsure of her feelings.

'Has Netta mentioned a key to you?'

Alice raised her eyebrows in surprise.

'I have only met Netta once. Is it something I should know about?'

'After my grandfather died she told me he kept a safety deposit box somewhere and that the key was very precious because the box contained valuable documents. My grandfather was a great authority on jade. Perhaps there is something about the turtle in it.'

'Have you asked Netta for this key?'

'She can be absent-minded and I think she may have forgotten where she put it.' Christine frowned. 'I am her, what do you call the term, *le plus proche parent?*'

'Next of kin?'

'Exactly. I do not wish to pry but I would like to know what has happened to this key. Netta will not tell me. Perhaps you could try asking her?'

Before Alice could reply, a noise from the bedroom above disturbed them.

'Ah, Netta is awake. I will go and see to her. You must come back another day.'

'I had an appointment with Netta today.' Alice stood her ground.

Christine delivered another of her charming smiles.

'Which I am now cancelling. *Au revoir.*'

Quite how it happened Alice did not know but moments later she found she

was standing on the farmhouse doorstep, the door firmly closed behind her.

Key to the Mystery?

In his cubby hole of an office David delved into the back of his desk.

'Is this what you are looking for?' He produced a key tied to a length of orange ribbon.

'You've got it?' Alice stifled her annoyance. It was difficult to be cross with David but he and Netta were pushing her tolerance level to its limit.

'Netta gave it to me for safe keeping. I have to admit I had forgotten about it.' David made one of his apologetic bows. 'I make no excuses. I like to lead a tranquil life. Lately there has been too much going on for me to cope with. I put the key away and dismissed it from my mind. Am I forgiven?'

Alice wished she could have the luxury of dismissing the jade turtle from her mind. It had caused her nothing but trouble.

'Of course,' she said in automatic response, her annoyance with David evaporating.

'I am so glad you dropped by.' David settled back happily into his creaky chair, 'Have you any news for me?'

After Alice had been summarily dismissed by Christine from Netta's farmhouse and hearing nothing further from Mike she had decided to call on David for no other reason than she enjoyed his company.

'Do you know what the key represents?' she asked. It felt heavy in Alice's hand. She turned it over but it contained no clue as to its purpose.

'It doesn't do to enquire too closely into Netta's private affairs.' David took a sip of his jasmine tea.

'Does Netta have a safe?' Alice pursued her line of questioning. It wasn't easy getting straight answers from David.

David inclined his head.

'I do not know. So sorry.'

He folded his hands into the sleeves

of his silk tunic and appeared to go into a trance. Reluctant to disturb his meditations, Alice finished her tea.

She could hear the chatter of the flower-arrangers in the room next door as she inhaled a light vanilla fragrance wafting through an open window. The Tao centre always provided an oasis of calm and that was why visiting David was such a pleasure. It was a haven of refuge far removed from the trials of day-to-day life.

David's voice lured Alice out of her daydream of flowers and exotic fragrances.

'How is Netta?' he asked.

'I didn't get to see her,' Alice admitted.

David made a mild gesture of annoyance.

'I try to live in harmony with everyone but at times she tests even my patience. A friendship should work both ways, don't you agree?'

Alice thought back to her relationship with Jack. He had more than tested her patience and as for being an equal partner in their relationship, equality was something Jack never seemed to have quite grasped.

'I'm not the one to advise you on that, David,' Alice said with a rueful smile. 'I've made too many bad decisions.'

'Ah, you are not in a good place at the moment but things will come right.' David patted her hand.

'How can you know that?' Alice did not share David's confidence in her future.

'Because you have inner strength and beauty,' he added.

'Excuse me?' Her mouth fell open in disbelief.

'Do not look so surprised. Why is there no time these days to appreciate the beauty of mind and spirit?' David's bright eyes were filled with sadness. 'It comes in so many forms but we live in a commercial world that only appreciates a flawless appearance. Beauty comes from the soul.' He closed his eyes for a moment as if composing himself.

'Like you, my dear Alice, I too have made wrong decisions but we must take great joy in learning from experience.' David opened his eyes and appeared to shake himself back to the present. 'I forget where we were,' he admitted.

'Netta's key,' Alice reminded him. 'Shouldn't you return it to her?'

'She is not talking to me.'

'If you really wanted to see her, nothing should stop you.'

'She hasn't asked for it back.'

'It sounds to me like you are making excuses,' Alice chided.

'How did you learn of the key's existence if you did not get to see Netta?' David enquired, seemingly unruffled by the teasing note of Alice's voice.

'Christine, her step granddaughter, answered the door and we had coffee together.'

'Christine is here?' A wary expression crossed David's face.

'Yes.'

'She is a troubled soul. Tell me what colour is her hair this week?'

'It's green and orange.'

'That is good.' David's mood swings were proving difficult to follow. 'Colour plays a great part in our personal yin and yang,' he explained. 'Green balances out the enthusiasm and stimulation of the creativity of the colour orange.'

'Then take Netta's key up to the farmhouse now,' Alice said, too baffled to ask David for an explanation. 'If Netta won't talk to you, you can return the key to Christine and have a good chat about yins and yangs.'

'I do not wish to entrust Christine with the key's safety,' David announced.

'Why ever not?'

'You are a better guardian,' David said, proving remarkably stubborn on that point. 'Your life is here in Saltwich.'

'I can't guarantee for how long.'

'Like the dog roses, you are a child of the hedgerows.'

Alice looked out of the window to where the sun sparkled on the meandering river where students punted up and down, laughing and calling out to each other as they grappled with their punt poles.

It would be a wrench to leave Saltwich but she wasn't sure she had ever thought of herself as a child of the hedgerows.

'The fretted stone of the college is so magnificent in the sunshine,' David continued. 'Look at that willow draped over the water and the serenity of the swans as they glide along.'

Alice blinked, lost for words.

'Your heart is here,' David insisted. 'Stay and be happy.'

'How can I with the shadow of guilt hanging over me?' Alice asked.

'If you are guilty then so am I.'

'It isn't your partner who is implicated in the theft of a turtle.'

'Your partner was unsuccessful in his endeavours. I was the one on duty when it disappeared. I share your guilt.'

'It's kind of you to say so, David.' Alice smiled at him. 'But you won't change my mind.'

'Please,' he persisted, 'will you look after Netta's key for me?'

'Netta entrusted you with its safety.'

'A trust I am now passing on to you.'

'Shouldn't you tell Netta you have given me the key?'

'Things will resolve themselves in time,' was David's enigmatic reply.

Too exhausted to think up further objections, Alice gave in and slipped the key into her bag. Somehow she would find an appropriate moment to return it to Netta.

'Have you heard any more about the whereabouts of the turtle?' she asked David.

'Its disappearance has not affected attendance levels.' David beamed at her. 'In fact, they are significantly up. Everyone wants to inspect the scene of the crime. I am thinking of going into the business of providing selfie sticks.' David chuckled. 'Don't you have a saying in English about clouds and silver linings?'

'And Lan?' Alice persisted, anxious to tie up all loose ends.

'Our paths have not crossed,' David replied with the enigmatic expression he always assumed when discussing Ms Nguyen. 'Have you heard anything?'

'She isn't picking up my calls, either,' Alice admitted. 'I can't understand it. She gave me forty-eight hours to come up with something otherwise she wanted her money back.'

'That is strange,' David agreed, 'but of one thing you can be sure, we haven't heard the last of Lan Nguyen.' He paused. 'Where is your friend Mike today?'

'In a business meeting.'

'Then why don't you go for a walk to clear your head? It seems a shame to waste a beautiful afternoon.'

'I haven't got time to go for a walk,' Alice objected.

'Haven't you?' David enquired.

Alice bit her lip.

'Physical activity stimulates the senses and it helps to embrace nature during a time of turmoil.'

'David, aren't you worried about the loss of the turtle?' Alice was mystified by his lack of emotion over its recent theft.

'Material possessions do not cause me any loss of sleep. The important things in life are available to everyone.'

'Such as dog roses and willows over the water?'

'What use would I have for an inanimate piece of jade?'

'It belonged to Netta and it has been stolen.'

'Do you see her here wondering where it could be?'

'No,' Alice had to agree.

'Then I speak the truth.'

'What about Selwyn Bishop?'

'He was the man reading his facts and figures, wasn't he?'

'Moments before the turtle disappeared.'

'He is a collector of rare and

beautiful pieces of art but I fear, like so many individuals, he knows the price of everything but the value of nothing.' David sighed then looked over his shoulder. 'The flower arranging session next door appears to be coming to an end. I have things to do. Please, Alice, take my advice and embrace some calm.'

Alice watched David scuttle away.

It had been a while since Alice had done a workout. Perhaps she needed to take David's advice. Physical activity would do her good.

She checked her mobile for messages. Nothing from Mike. His meeting with Venetia appeared to be taking all day.

'I'm about to go off duty,' Terry, the fitness centre manager, greeted Alice, 'but you're welcome to use the equipment. Make sure you turn the lights out after you. Important family party,' he explained, 'which I dare not miss or I run the risk of incurring the wrath of my in-laws. *Ciao*.'

Towelling her hair dry after her

shower and fitness workout, Alice shrugged on her clothes then repressed a shiver. Her footsteps echoed around the deserted gym and pool area. The equipment loomed menacingly at her creating eerie shadows on the wall.

She paused by the water cooler and placing a beaker under the spout waited for it to fill up. Glancing over her shoulder she couldn't shake off the suspicion that she wasn't alone. In the background she heard a faint click.

'Who's there?' she called out.

Her beaker of water slipped from her fingers as the gym was plunged into darkness.

Dark Discovery

Desperately trying to remember her self-defence disciplines, Alice lashed out at the shadow emerging from the darkness. Her fist came into contact with something solid. A grunt and a loud curse were followed by a dull thud as her victim hit the ground.

Alice planted her foot firmly on the writhing body. The hammering of her heartbeat was making it difficult to breathe.

Her assailant attempted to escape from the weight of her foot. Struggling to keep her balance Alice wobbled then increased the pressure.

Firm fingers encircled her ankle. To her horror she realised one tug could bring her to her knees. Lights from the next-door hotel twinkled in the darkness.

'Help!' she yelled at the top of her voice.

'Shut up.'

'Help, someone, anyone! I'm being attacked!'

The fingers continued to grip her ankle like bands of iron.

'You'll get us both arrested if you don't zip it.'

'Mike?' Alice stuttered as a further protest died in her throat.

He released his hold on her ankle.

'What are you doing creeping around in the dark?'

'Look, have you got a flashlight? I can't see a thing.'

Alice retrieved her mobile and shone the torch on to the floor as Mike struggled into a semi upright position and rubbed his forehead.

'What are you playing at — turning out the lights?' Alice demanded.

'I didn't.'

'I don't believe you.'

'Give me one good reason why I should.'

'If you didn't, who did?'

'You tell me.'

She peered at him in the half-light. There was a large streak of dirt on his forehead where he'd come into contact with the floor.

Conscience-stricken, Alice extended a hand and dragged Mike to his feet, keeping her torch trained on him as he dusted himself down.

'Why don't I check the fuse box?' he suggested. 'Then we can continue this healthy exchange in a decent light.'

'The control panel is by the entrance.'

Mike strode off and Alice steadied her balance by clinging on to the water cooler. The trees outside danced to the wind's eerie tune in a ghostly formation, their branches tapping accompaniment on the window.

'Success,' Mike's muffled voice announced from the depths of the control panel.

Alice shielded her eyes against the harsh electric light.

'That's better.' Mike was back at her side. 'What say we have a refreshing glass of water and talk things through?'

'You go first,' Alice insisted as they perched on adjacent exercise balls.

Mike sipped his water.

'David told me you were going for a workout.'

'Are you spinning me another line?' Alice narrowed her eyes.

'Now what are you accusing me of?'

Alice knew she was being unreasonable. It wasn't Mike's fault he was Jack's brother but Jack had told her so many tall stories she never knew what to believe.

Not for the first time she wished Mike didn't look quite so like Jack. Even with his shirt covered in dust and a lump the size of an egg on his forehead the resemblance was unmistakeable. Alice dug her fingernails into the palms of her hands. The sensation helped her to focus.

'David didn't know I would be here.'

'If you're not even going to bother to listen to me, I'm wasting my time,' Mike retaliated.

'It's just that David suggested I go for a walk.'

'Perhaps he can read people's minds, I don't know. Anyway, do you want to hear what I have to say?'

'Go on,' Alice relented, already regretting her outburst.

'When I got here the door was unlocked. I called out but didn't get a reply.'

'I was in the shower,' Alice explained.

Mike rubbed his head then winced as his fingers came into contact with the bump.

'What happened afterwards is a bit of a blur. I remember sensing movement behind me. I turned round and the next minute the lights went out.'

'Go on.'

'I was convinced I wasn't alone. I began creeping around, disorientated, because my eyes hadn't adjusted to the darkness. You came at me from nowhere and before I knew it I was seeing stars and pinned down by your delicate foot.'

'You shouldn't lunge out at people.'

'Neither should you,' Mike retorted.

'You don't think whoever blacked us out is still here, do you?' Alice glanced nervously over his shoulder.

'If they are I'll put them on to you.'

'Mike, I'm serious. What is going on?'

'Someone is after something.' He fixed his eyes on Alice's throat. 'I hate to seem inquisitive . . . ' he began.

'But?' Alice urged when he lapsed into silence.

'What's the significance of the orange ribbon hanging from your neck?'

Alice looked down.

'There's a key attached to it,' she explained.

'I can see that. What's it doing there?'

'I didn't want to lose it. It seemed easier to keep it round my neck.'

'Why?'

Alice shrugged.

'I don't know why, I just did it. That's all.'

'It's not the key to the gym, is it?'

'No, it belongs to Netta.'

'Do you think she's the reason the lights went out?'

'Has that bang on the head addled your brains or something?' Alice demanded. 'Netta's at home, probably tucked up in bed.'

'What's the key for?' Mark asked in a patient voice.

'I don't know and neither does David but he was looking after it for Netta. He gave it to me for safe keeping.'

'Why?'

'It's a long story.' Alice took a deep breath. 'Christine mentioned something about it when I went to visit Netta this morning.'

'Who's Christine?'

'Her grandmother was Claud's first wife.'

'I didn't know he had been married twice.'

'Neither did I.'

Mike looked thoughtful.

'I'm with you so far, I think. Claud was an investigative journalist, wasn't he?'

'So was Netta.'

'Do you think there's a possibility one of them discovered something significant?'

'What if they did?'

'Claud was an expert on jade, wasn't he? Did he keep records?'

'I have no idea about anything any more. This whole thing is getting beyond a joke,' Alice said. 'I didn't want the key. David virtually forced the wretched thing on me and if it represents a state secret then I am none the wiser.'

'Do you think someone else is after it? Someone who knows what it represents?'

'I don't know.'

'What did Netta tell you about it?'

Alice sighed.

'I didn't see her. I only spoke to Christine.'

'Then let's have another guess.'

'I'm not up to mind games at the moment. All I want to do is clear Jack's debt then draw a line under the whole affair. Jade turtles and cultural injustices do not feature in my life plan.'

'I told you I'll help you,' Mike insisted, 'and I will — but you're not making it easy for me.'

'What was that?' Alice tensed.

'I didn't hear anything.'

'Did you lock the door after you reset the trip switch?'

'It closed automatically.'

'That doesn't mean it's locked.'

'Stay here.' Mike stood up.

'I'm coming with you.'

'Don't you ever do what you're told?' Mike protested.

'I don't have to.' Alice barged past him, causing him to lose his footing.

'Watch out,' he yelled as for the second time that night the lights went out.

Alice tripped over a stray exercise ball and collided with a pair of feet. In the distance she heard a door bang.

Threatened at Gunpoint

'Lights going on,' Mike shouted and flicked the switch. 'Alice,' he ran towards the water cooler and knelt down beside her on the floor, 'are you hurt?'

'It's not here.' She pushed him away in frustration.

'Have you been injured?' he insisted, his eyes searching her face.

'The key, it was round my neck and now it's gone.'

Mike sat back on his heels then picked something up off the floor.

'Is this it?' He dangled a length of orange ribbon in front of her.

Alice snatched it from his grasp.

'The key's missing.'

'Never mind the key.' Mike touched Alice on the shoulder. 'Are you OK?'

'No, I'm not,' Alice retaliated, 'I'm fuming. Why didn't you check the door was locked behind you?'

'Because I didn't think someone would come in and start attacking us. This is sleepy Saltwich.'

'Sorry.' Alice tightened her hold on the piece of ribbon she was still clutching. 'Did you see anything?' she asked in a more composed voice.

'Such as?'

'Someone running away?'

'No, but we're dealing with someone who knows the rules.'

'I'm not sure what that means,' Alice responded with a shaky smile.

'It means the key holds some significance but for the life of me I can't think what it can be.'

'And whoever attacked us knew what the key was for.'

'Which puts them one up on us, doesn't it?'

'It's Netta's key. Do you think they could go after her next?'

'Didn't you say Christine was with her?'

'Yes.'

'And is Christine staying over?'

'I don't know,' Alice admitted. 'Mike,' she clutched his arm, 'Netta could be out at the farmhouse on her own.'

'Lock up here.' He leaped to his feet. 'You'd better leave the gym key at reception in case they've got ideas of coming back.'

'What shall I say about the break in?'

'Nothing. They don't appear to have taken anything apart from your key and we don't want to start a panic.'

Mike was already revving up his engine as Alice raced across the car park and jumped in the passenger seat. He reversed, spun the steering wheel in the opposite direction then headed out of the gates, all in one manoeuvre.

'What could be so important about a key that someone risks attacking us?' Alice clutched the dashboard as Mike took a bend in the road at breakneck speed.

'Whoever took it must know what it's for.'

'Proof of the turtle's provenance?' Alice hazarded a guess. 'Hidden away somewhere?'

'And if that proof is in Netta's house?' Mike glanced at Alice.

'Surely it's not worth attacking Netta for a piece of paper.'

'Who's to know what they might do? They weren't afraid of attacking us.'

'Can't you go any faster?' Alice demanded.

The engine note deepened as Mike put his foot down.

'I'm convinced David knows something he's not telling us.'

'See if you can raise him.'

'I don't think he checks voicemail and he hardly ever switches on. He'll probably be meditating in front of a candle or something.'

'When are that pair going to grow up?' Mike hit the steering in frustration.

'I like David,' Alice protested. 'He's kind hearted and gentle.'

'And Netta reminds me of you,' Mike said with a trace of a smile in his voice.

'What exactly have I got in common with Netta?'

'You can both be infuriating — and independent.'

'There's nothing wrong with being independent.' Alice turned her head to the window and watched the trees race by as they sped along.

'I agree.'

'And I am not infuriating.'

'We'll leave that one for another time, shall we? Come on,' he muttered under his breath as a learner driver pulled out in front of them, 'this is no time to be taking a driving lesson.'

'Stop hassling them,' Alice was still clutching the dashboard, 'we don't want to wind up in a ditch.'

'That's the least of our problems,' Mike said as the driver continued to trundle along in front of them.

'I don't suppose there's anything from Jack?' Alice asked in the vain hope that Mike might have heard from his brother.

''Fraid not,' he replied.

The learner driver turned off in the direction of the academy and Mike increased his speed.

'Right here,' Alice instructed, causing Mike to do another racing turn on protesting tyres and incurring the wrath of the vehicle behind them.

'Sorry,' Mike flashed his hazards in apology as they commenced their bumpy drive down the lane that led to Netta's remote farmhouse. 'Can you see anything?'

'We're still a way off.'

'Why does Netta have to live in the middle of nowhere?' he complained.

'Netta can't be involved in stealing her own turtle, can she?'

Mike swerved as he took his eyes off the road.

'Anything's possible but I can't see it myself. Whoever attacked you must have known the key was in your possession.'

'How? David only gave it to me today and it couldn't have been him.'

'Maybe I was right and someone was

following me and heard us talking about it in the gym.'

'It could have been Lan, I suppose,' Alice thought about it, 'but the scent was all wrong.'

'I beg your pardon?'

'Lan wore a fragrance that reminded me of jasmine and rose petals. Besides, David said she always got other people to do her dirty work. We're on the wrong track,' Alice said.

'I don't think so.'

'I mean you have taken a wrong turn. We should have gone left back there.'

Mike thrust the controls into reverse gear, righted the car and drove back the way they'd come.

'There,' Alice squinted through the windscreen. Mike's headlights arced the front of the farmhouse. 'I don't see Christine's car.'

Mike gave several loud blasts of his horn.

'What did you do that for?'

'To warn Netta of our arrival.'

'If I know Netta she won't take

kindly to being disturbed by the blast of a horn.'

'She may have no choice,' Mike said in grim reply. 'See if you can raise her.'

Alice jumped out of the car.

'Stay where you are.' A figure had appeared in the doorway — wielding a gun.

'Netta,' Alice stumbled in relief, 'thank goodness you're safe.'

'Don't move. I've got you covered.'

'Netta it's me, Alice.'

'Who's that with you?'

'Mike. You met him at the yellow party. He was wearing a tangerine tie.'

'What are you doing here?'

'We came to see if you were all right.' Mike joined Alice.

'I don't like unexpected visitors and I've had my fill of them tonight.'

'You've had other visitors?' Alice was quick to pick up on that statement.

'Indeed I have.'

'Who?'

'They didn't say.'

'Is Christine here?'

'An emergency came up, she had to leave.'

'Netta,' Mike coaxed, 'now you've established who we are, may we come in?'

'Why?'

'We have some news for you,' Alice said.

Netta looked hard at them both then lowered her weapon.

'Old Faithful's not loaded,' she confided.

Alice expelled a sigh of relief.

'Maybe not but it doesn't do to go waving it around at people,' Mike stepped forward and relieved her of the gun, 'and have you got a licence?'

'Don't need one,' Netta confided. 'It's made of wood, see? Claud used it to good effect on our travels. It fooled everybody. It even fooled you, didn't it?'

'All the same, you can't go round threatening people.'

'I didn't. You were on my property without my permission and when I need a lecture on personal safety I'll ask for one. What have you been up to? You look like you've been in the wars. That's quite a lump on your forehead.'

'We'll tell you about it inside.'

'What do you want with me anyway?'

'Come on, Netta,' Mike ushered her towards the front door, 'it's getting cold out here.'

'I'd like a cup of tea,' Netta admitted.

'Let's go then.'

Mike added coal to the log fire burning in the grate while Alice sorted out the tea.

With the curtains drawn against the encroaching night sky and the flames from the fire taking hold of the fresh coal, Alice's anxieties about Netta's safety faded.

'Right, then — what's all this about?' Netta asked.

'Why don't you tell us first what happened to you?' Mike invited Netta to go first.

'After I waved Christine off I came back in here and had a snooze. Her

140

visits always tire me out. She's got so much restless energy. When I woke up I heard a disturbance outside. One or two of the local farm lads like to keep an eye on me so I called out that I was in here.'

'Go on,' Alice urged.

'When there was no response I decided to investigate.'

'Don't you realise how dangerous that was?'

'Stuff and nonsense,' Netta rebuffed his concern. 'I've been in scrapes before and I dare say I'll encounter a few more.' She made an agitated gesture with her hand, 'Where was I?'

'The disturbance outside,' Alice prompted.

'I grabbed up Old Faithful and peered through my spy hole in the door.'

'What did you see?' Alice was having difficulty containing her impatience.

'A car.'

'Did it have more than one passenger?' Mike asked.

'Difficult to be sure.'

'What did they want?'

'I don't know,' Netta paused, 'but I decided I didn't like the look of them. I shouted out that they weren't welcome and if they weren't off the premises in two minutes I was calling the police.'

'You didn't scare them off with a fake gun?' Alice demanded.

'I didn't open the door but then when I heard you coming down the drive blasting your horn I thought it was them coming back. I decided enough was enough.'

'We didn't pass anyone on the way down,' Alice said in a low voice to Mike. 'They could still be hanging around.'

Netta stifled a yawn.

'I'm tired. I want you to leave now.'

'One more thing before we go,' Mike said.

'Yes?'

'We think all this could be to do with the jade turtle.'

'That wretched thing! Claud always

said it was cursed and I'm beginning to believe him.'

'Do you know anyone who would want to steal it?'

'Lan Nguyen, Selwyn Bishop, David.' Netta's eyelids began to flutter.

'We're tiring her out,' Alice mouthed to Mike.

'You're right. She's not making sense. David wouldn't steal the turtle. We'll find our own way out.' He touched Netta's arm but she had already fallen asleep.

* * *

'I don't like leaving Netta on her own,' Alice said as they drove away from the farmhouse after having done a quick search of the outhouses to make sure no-one was still hanging around.

'She'll be quite safe,' Mike reassured her. 'While you were checking the hen coop I managed to get hold of David.'

'What can he do?'

'Look after Netta, and he does need to be kept in the loop even if he is holding out on us.'

'You know if he turns up on her doorstep she won't let him in.'

'He has a key.'

'What?'

'He only just told me.'

'It would have saved us a lot of hassle if he'd volunteered that piece of information earlier.'

'You know David. Practical stuff like keys passes him by.'

'How many of Netta's keys has he got in his possession?'

'You could try asking him,' Mike suggested.

'Sometimes I think he and Netta live on a different planet from the rest of us.'

'I'm beginning to feel the same. I mean, all this talk about the turtle being cursed. It's straight out of a dime novel. We both need a break,' Mike agreed. 'Fancy a trip on the water tomorrow for the ceremony of the floats?'

'I don't think so.'

'There are going to be dragons and fairy lights and a display of water sports and all sorts of other stuff.'

'I'm not sure I'm in the mood for that sort of thing.'

'There'll be loads of students out for a good time. It's exactly what we both need to lighten up.'

'I know you're doing your best to make things better for me, Mike, and don't think I'm not grateful.'

'Go on,' Mike urged.

'There are one or two things you need to know. Please, hear me out,' she stalled Mike as he attempted to interrupt. 'Jack left me in debt — serious debt. I don't have the luxury of a family allowance to fall back on. I am in it up to my neck and that's why I don't want to play water fairies.'

'Hey!' Mike looked concerned. 'What's brought this on?'

'I can't carry on the agency without Jack. I don't have the funds. For all I

145

know, this situation has affected my credit rating so I can't set up another agency under a new name. I've no idea what other deals Jack set up behind my back. Also, I suspect I am shortly going to be homeless.'

'Who says?'

'It's only a matter of time before these accountants of yours will want me out of the studio complex.'

'I have no issues with you staying there and I'm sure Jack wouldn't have any either.'

'Maybe not,' Alice conceded, 'but I can't stay on for ever.'

'Think of it as family compensation.'

'Haven't you listened to a word I've said?' Alice raised her voice.

'You're being stubborn like Netta.'

'I am not being stubborn,' Alice gritted her teeth. 'Get real, Mike. Jack is a lovely guy but this time someone's got to make good on his debts and it looks like it's got to be me.'

They drove in silence for a few minutes before Mike spoke.

'I wasn't going to tell you this,' he began. The tone of his voice quickened Alice's pulse.

'More bad news?' she asked in a hollow voice.

'It concerns my meeting with Venetia.'

'The family accountant?' Alice knew she sounded bitter but she couldn't help it.

'This isn't easy for me because I suspect you are going to blow your top.' An angry frown creased Mike's brow.

'Drop me here,' Alice said.

'There's no need to overreact.'

'I'm not. This is where I left my car, remember?'

Mike drew into the hotel car park.

'I'll follow you back to the studio.'

'Why?'

'What I have to say is important. Now are you with me or do I park outside the studio all night and start making a nuisance of myself? And don't think I don't mean it.'

Alice sighed, accepting the inevitable.

'I'll leave the door open. You know the way up.'

★ ★ ★

'Don't worry, I won't stay long.' Mike perched on a kitchen stool.

Alice remained standing. Sitting down would put her at a direct disadvantage.

'So . . . your accountant?' she prompted.

'Venetia and her husband used to deal with our family affairs, then after she was widowed she continued on her own. She's more like a family friend.'

'Is this important?' Alice queried with a frown.

'She's been aware of Jack's lack of financial understanding for many years.'

'You mean she's bailed him out?'

'I wouldn't have put it quite like that.'

The harsh strip lighting emphasised the dark circles under Mike's eyes.

'I'm sorry,' Alice apologised. 'I didn't

mean to doubt Venetia's integrity. I'm sure she's always acted in your family's best interests.'

'What I'm trying to say is that after going through all the figures Venetia has come up with a solution to our problem.'

'Our problem?' Alice raised an eyebrow.

'Venetia informs me there is enough credit in Jack's emergency fund for the agency to continue.' Mike paused. 'She can work it but she would prefer a member of the family to be on board.'

Alice closed her eyes. She should have expected something like this.

'The family member being you, I suppose.'

'There is no-one else,' Mike admitted, 'but you don't have to make a decision right now. If you like I could arrange an appointment for you to discuss the situation with Venetia. She's much better at explaining things than I am.'

'I'll think about it,' Alice acquiesced.

'Good. I'll pick you up at ten o'clock.'

The touch of his lips on her cheek was so gentle Alice wasn't sure she had imagined it. Watching from the kitchen window she didn't move until the tail-lights of Mike's car disappeared into the evening mist.

Rocking the Boat

Myriad themed floats sailed down the river to the accompaniment of the brass band playing on the summer pavilion lawn.

Members of the committee were decked out in roaring Twenties outfits and the graceful Tao centre attendants sported the bright peacock silk colours showcasing their heritage. As they flitted from guest to guest offering refreshments they reminded Alice of the exotic birds she and Jack had seen on their cruise through the islands of the South China Sea.

'Do you want to have a go in a punt?' Alice asked Mike as they stood on the riverbank.

'I, er . . . ' Mike hesitated.

'It's for charity and didn't we agree we needed a change?'

'Yes,' Mike conceded.

'Then now's your chance,' Alice tugged at his sleeve. 'It's this way.'

'Do we have to dress up?' Mike looked less than enthusiastic as Alice urged him towards the boathouse.

'How about wearing this?' Alice produced a hat from the costume box and adjusted the scarlet and yellow ribbon circling the brim of the straw boater.

'This would suit you, too.' With delicate butterfly movements a Tao attendant produced a striped blazer from the bottom of a wicker basket and shook it out. 'You try it on, please?'

'What are you going to wear?' Mike adjusted the brim of his boater to a more rakish angle.

'In that dress, the lady looks lovely as she is.' The boatman blew her a kiss from his riverside hut. 'Don't forget your quant, sir.'

'My what?'

A group of chattering assistants gathered round him and a pole was thrust into Mike's hands.

'Use it carefully and it'll steer you along nicely,' the boatman advised.

'You must have your photo taken, too.' An attendant clad in a vivid shade of orange silk flashed her camera in their direction. 'For the records, and,' she added with a gentle smile, 'you may even win a wonderful prize.'

'Let's hope it's not a turtle,' Mike muttered under his breath. 'Right,' he straightened his shoulders, 'where do we go and what do we do?'

Alice led him across the rickety bridge to where the punts were moored. Mike handed over his donation.

'I've never done this sort of thing before,' he confided to Alice.

'Want me to go first?' she offered.

'I'll see what I can do and if I make a fool of myself you can take over.'

'Good luck, honoured lady and gentleman.'

A Tao assistant sprinkled yellow petals over the water from suspended straw baskets and, placing the palms of her hands together, bowed.

'One, two, three, off you go.' The boatman nudged their punt into the water.

Alice leaned against the embroidered cushions and watched Mike handle the pole with surprising dexterity, skilfully avoiding the overhanging willows and the inquisitive ducks quacking around them. She closed her eyes. In the distance the clock in the church tower struck midday.

'This is like a scene out of a classic novel.' Mike's voice broke into Alice's thoughts.

'Mmm,' she agreed, lazily trailing her hand in the water. 'How's it going?'

'It's not as easy as it looks,' Mike complained. 'You have to sort of twirl the quant round then pull it up and out. Trouble is the water's a bit sticky down below.' He peered into its swirling depths.

'Don't worry — you won't drown if you do fall in.' Alice laughed.

'What made you say that?'

The urgency in Mike's voice startled Alice.

'No reason, really.' She paused. 'Do you have issues with water?' she asked, noting the mild panic on Mike's face.

A sudden jolt rocked their punt. Mike windmilled his arms in the air before falling backwards and landing in the water with an undignified yell.

'Mike!' Alice shrieked.

'Sorry,' a harassed father tried to dislodge his punt from theirs, 'it's my first time at this sort of thing.'

'Here, grab a hold of this.' A spectator offered Mike an oar as he resurfaced and began desperately paddling to keep afloat.

Trying to steady her punt, Alice grabbed out at an overhanging branch but she was too late and it broke away in her hands.

'We come.' A group of agitated hostesses ran along the riverbank in their traditional costumes, doing their best not to trip over the long hems.

'Keep the camera rolling, this is great

footage,' Alice heard a voice in the background instruct a television crew from a local news station.

'I can't swim.' Mike flailed around in the water.

'Not deep.' A hostess flapped her hands at him.

Alice felt another bump. Her punt had run aground on a shallow bank. Jumping on to the grass she scrambled towards Mike.

'Stand up,' she shouted then waded into the water.

'My feet are stuck.' His breath was coming in short sharp bursts.

With the help of a band of volunteers Mike was prised out of the mud and on to the grass to where the emergency health and safety crew were waiting for them with a stretcher.

'There's no need for that. It's only mud,' Alice insisted.

'We have to check you over,' the senior officer produced foil blankets, 'for shock.'

'Then we'll walk.'

'The gentleman has a nasty bump on his head.'

'He did that yesterday.'

'We don't want him suffering from concussion.'

'I should have told you water isn't my thing,' Mike mumbled as they were led away to the first aid tent.

'Instead you decided to play the big hero and pretend you were cool with water?' Alice shook her head. 'What is it with men?'

'It's because of Jack,' Mike admitted reluctantly.

'You can't blame this one on him.'

'Sit down.' A motherly woman bustled around. 'My, you have been in the wars. I've got a brew on the go and a bag of doughnuts. Sugar is good for shock.'

'Why because of Jack?' Alice prompted as they nursed two mugs of strong tea.

'He was the sporty one. He took after our father, coming first in all the races, picked for the school football team, great at water sports, captain of everything going.'

'I can imagine,' Alice said.

'One day Jack said he'd give me a swimming lesson. It was an accident,' Mike insisted.

'What was?' Alice asked in a careful voice.

'I went under. I panicked. Jack . . . ' Mike paused. 'He wasn't scared of anything. He thought the whole thing was funny.'

'Did he tell you it was important to face up to your fears?'

'Later,' Mike admitted, 'after he eventually rescued me, but it doesn't seem to have worked.'

With damp hair plastered to his head and shivering in his foil blanket Mike looked nothing like the man who had strode into the wet cafe a few days ago to break the news to her that Jack was married.

'Ridiculous, isn't it?' Mike said when Alice didn't speak. 'To be scared of water.'

'No, it isn't,' she insisted.

'But you were right, it's not Jack's fault I can't swim.'

'Maybe not, but Jack works by a different set of rules. If things don't work out for him he moves on and leaves someone else to sort out the mess.

'It's the same with facing up to your fears. He's not afraid of anything so he doesn't understand. He can be kind,' Alice was quick to point out, 'and generous, but at times not very thoughtful. You're — different.'

'Good different or bad different?' Mike sounded more like his usual self.

Alice blinked, not sure where her pep talk was going.

'Just different,' she said.

'Thanks for that. Want one?' Mike mumbled and picking up the plate of doughnuts offered them to her with an embarrassed smile.

Alice accepted one then laughed as strawberry jam squirted through her fingers.

'You're different too.' Mike watched her lick it off her hands. 'In fact you're quite unlike anyone I've ever met before.'

'Am I?' Alice's voice was almost drowned out by the sound of brass band music drifting up from the river.

'And,' he leaned in closer towards her, 'You've got sugar on your chin.'

Alice rubbed the palm of her hand across her face before Mike could do it for her.

'It sounds like they're cheering the winners home,' she said, anxious to defuse the situation.

'I'm pretty certain we've been disqualified. I wonder what became of our punt.'

'I hope someone rescued it, and your quant.'

'Last I saw it was merrily heading downstream.' The light caught the freckles on Mike's forehead as the rest of his face creased into a smile.

'Perhaps,' Alice swallowed the last of her doughnut, 'we ought to go outside and see what's going on?'

Mike shrugged off his foil blanket.

'I suppose we should, if only to be good sports and congratulate the winners. Is that your mobile?'

'What have you been up to?' a voice demanded down the line as Alice answered her call.

Trapped!

'Netta?' Alice raised her eyebrows at Mike who was looking questioningly at her.

'You're on the local news.'

'What?'

Mike jumped at the sound of Alice's raised voice.

'Netta's OK, isn't she? I mean she hasn't been attacked in the night or anything?'

'We're on television.'

'Television?'

It was Mike's turn to shout. Netta guffawed down the line.

'Mike does look ridiculous flapping around in the water like a demented seal and shouting his head off. Not one of nature's water babies, is he? And you rescued him, Alice — girl power!'

Netta had a carrying voice and Mike groaned as he overheard her vivid description of his fall.

'It wasn't like that.' Alice did her best to stall Netta, who was having none of it and continued to find the situation more than amusing.

'I haven't had such a good laugh in weeks.'

'Netta.' Alice took a deep breath. 'I need to run some things past you again. We were all tired last night and . . . '

'What the . . . ?' Netta gasped in surprise.

'What's happening? Netta?' Alice prompted when there was no response, 'Are you there?'

'Lan Nguyen.'

'What about her?'

'There, on the river bank lurking in the undergrowth. I have to record this. Where's the remote when you need it?' Netta made a noise of frustration. 'Too late, she's disappeared. You'll have to take my word for it.'

'Are you sure it was Lan?'

'Plain as day and I'm convinced she

was talking to that shadowy creature Selwyn Bishop.'

Mike was now making frantic gestures at Alice.

'Updates,' he urged.

'Netta thinks she saw Lan.'

'I don't think I saw her,' Netta bellowed down the line. 'I know I saw her.'

'Netta,' Alice interrupted in a firm voice, 'the key you gave David for safe keeping?'

'What was that? Why doesn't this wretched machine record?'

'Are you listening to me?' Alice demanded.

'Yes.' It was obvious from the tone of Netta's voice that she was being economical with the truth.

'What did I just say?'

'Um,' Netta hesitated, 'something about Mike falling in the water?'

'The key you gave David,' Alice repeated patiently.

'Did you tell David to keep an eye on me?' she demanded. 'He turned up here late last night you know. We had a cup of one of his herbal teas and then I sent him packing. I don't need a nanny.' Her voice softened. 'But it was good to see him. I wouldn't have opened the door but he let himself in. Gave me a bit of a shock, I can tell you. Is that the key you are referring to?' she asked.

'Christine mentioned a key. It might have belonged to Claud?'

'What business is it of hers?' Netta sounded affronted.

'What is it for? And don't pretend you don't know.'

'If you must know, Claud kept his research locked up in a deposit box. Why are you so interested in a key, for heaven's sake? You should be out chasing Lan and her partner in crime. I've pointed you in the right direction.'

'David gave me your key.'

'Was that them again? Hey, I think it was. I caught a glimpse of scarlet silk.'

'Netta, will you turn the television off?' Alice demanded in as patient a voice as she could manage.

'If I must,' Netta replied in a sulky voice. 'They've stopped covering the ceremony anyway and moved on to some boring journalistic conference. Look at all those people staring at screens. I was much more hands on.

'Did I tell you about the time I was taken hostage on New Year's Eve because some tribal leader was offended when I turned down his offer to become one of his wives?

'That was a bit scary but after some diplomatic pressure we came to an amicable solution. Where were we?' Netta finally ground to a halt with her reminiscences.

'Claud's key? Christine was wondering where it was.'

'She had no reason to.' There was now a note of suspicion in Netta's voice. 'What's her agenda?'

'The thing is . . . ' Alice tried to continue with her explanation but was again thwarted by a distracted Netta.

'I think Selwyn Bishop is behind all this. My guess is he wants the jade turtle for his wretched collection and that Lan has promised to get it for him but he won't go ahead with the purchase unless she can provide a genuine provenance.'

'Are you saying Claud's papers represent this provenance?'

'I'm not saying anything.'

'Netta, this is important. Where did Claud keep his papers?'

'Give me that phone.' Mike made to grab it from Alice who stepped backwards. Losing her balance, her mobile sprang from her fingers and landed in a muddy patch of grass.

'What are you playing at?' Alice demanded.

'Why didn't you tell Netta we lost the key because someone attacked us?'

'I was about to before you butted in. Netta will think I've cut the call and now I can't get a signal.'

'What was all that about Lan?'

'According to Netta she's around here somewhere.'

'Doing what?'

'I've no idea but she was with Selwyn Bishop.'

'We need to get back to the ceremony.'

More people were now milling around and Alice looked at Mike in despair.

'We'll never find Lan in this crowd and I wouldn't know what to say to her even if we did.'

'A face to face is exactly what's needed,' Mike insisted. 'I've had enough of all this subterfuge.'

'You are recovered?' David was standing behind them, his benign smile lighting up his face. 'We have been watching the news in the press tent. The media coverage has been extra special.' David moved closer to Mike.

'You do not like water? I sympathise. It plays a significant role in our culture but I cannot say I enjoy wading around in it. I saw too many rice paddies as a child. After a while water loses its attraction.'

'I can't come up with such a good

excuse,' Mike admitted.

'You do not need to excuse yourself at all and don't worry about the punt, everything has been returned to the boatman. He is reporting an increase in business due to the publicity so something good came of the incident.'

'Netta said she saw Lan Nguyen on the riverbank with Selwyn Bishop.' Alice elbowed into the conversation.

'It is possible but with so many visitors I doubt very much if we would be able to track her down.' David paused. 'I'm not sure I want to speak to her anyway.'

'Everyone seems to be forgetting we need to find the turtle,' Alice said.

'Material possessions do not interest me.'

'You were supposed to be keeping an eye on it,' Alice reminded David.

'It will turn up,' he replied with maddening equanimity.

'Would you have any idea where Claud would keep a safety deposit box?' Mike asked.

'Why do you need to know such a thing?'

'That key you gave Alice?'

'I remember.'

'Yesterday we were attacked and it was taken from us,' Mike explained.

'Someone attacked you?' David asked in alarm, clasping Alice's hand in his. 'Is that how you got the bump on your head?'

'That's not the point.' Mike glossed over his explanation before Alice could confess to her part in the incident.

'All this violence,' David still looked upset. 'You must be careful.'

'What we want to know is why is the safety deposit box so significant?' Mike prompted.

'And who knew I had the key?' Alice added.

David held up his hands.

'One at a time, please,' he said.

'You were friends with Claud. Did he give you any idea where he might have kept his valuables?' Mike persisted.

A fleeting look Alice did not understand crossed David's face before he seemed to come to a decision.

'You had better come with me.'

'Where to?' Mike demanded.

'Back to the centre.'

Progress was difficult with crowds of people clustering around Mike.

'You're trending on social media. You won't believe the number of hits you've had.' An excited youngster waved his device at them. 'Can I have a selfie?'

Alice watched Mike stand patiently at the head of a line of festival-goers to have his picture taken with student after student followed by several of the officials and a final one for the television station who were responsible for the original video recording.

Yet again Alice was struck by how different Mike was from his brother. Jack loved being the centre of attention but patience was not one of his virtues. He would have been unable to stand still for so long and repeatedly answer the same questions but Mike's smile didn't slip as he admitted his issue with water. Eventually he cast Alice an imploring look.

'OK, thanks everyone.' She stepped forward. 'We have to go now.' Her words were followed by a good-natured protest. 'Mr Liu is a very busy man. We can't keep him waiting any longer.'

David bowed courteously at the students.

'Thank you so much, my young friends. Enjoy the rest of your day.'

The Tao centre was deserted as David unlocked the door.

'By the way, Netta and I are back on speaking terms.'

'She told us,' Alice replied.

'I have been so worried about her. She is such a dear person.'

Their footsteps echoed over the stone floor as David led them down back corridors to an area not usually open to the public.

'I had no idea this place was so big,' Alice said as David paused by a heavy door. It was ajar and he pushed it open.

'What is this, a storeroom?' Mike followed him through and looked around.

Old-fashioned furniture stood side by side next to broken heaters and discarded office equipment. The smell of dust caused Alice to sneeze violently.

'I should have warned you,' David apologised. 'No-one comes down here any more. It is such a waste of valuable space but with economic cutbacks there is no need for these rooms. I fear this part of the building may be knocked down and the land used for another purpose.' He inspected a bank of functional grey lockers.

'I discovered these when I was doing an inventory for the authorities. I believe they have been here a long time, probably from when personal belongings were locked away on a daily basis.

'We now use filing cabinets in the central office for any valuables. All the lockers have individual numbers and keys so when Claud mentioned he was looking for somewhere to store his papers I suggested he put them here. It's as safe a place as anywhere.'

'Do you know the number of Claud's locker?' Mike asked.

'If I did I am afraid I have misplaced it.'

A draught of air behind them caused Alice to turn round. The door to the storeroom slammed shut.

'That is very annoying,' David said.

'What happened there?' Mike looked over his shoulder.

'Do you think we were being followed again?' Alice asked.

'I do not know but what I do know is that the door is self locking and can only be opened from the outside.'

'You mean we're trapped?' Mike faced David.

'Yes — and no-one will know where we are.'

The Great Escape

'No worries, we'll call up for help.' Mike looked hopefully at Alice.

'I damaged my mobile when I dropped it in the mud.'

Mike pulled a face.

'And I lost mine in the water — not that there's much chance of getting a signal in here.'

Alice pressed a couple of buttons on her mobile but the keypad refused to respond to her touch. A faint moan drew Mike's attention to the corner of the room.

'For goodness' sake, David, now is not the time to start chanting.' He bent over the slumped form. 'David?' He shook him by the shoulder. David's head fell forward. 'David,' Mike repeated in a raised voice, 'can you hear me?'

'Never give in to weakness.' David's eyelids fluttered.

'David, it's me, Mike, and Alice. Stay with us.'

'Loosen his jacket,' Alice suggested.

'I think he's having a panic attack.'

'Are you sure? He always seems so calm to me.'

'Maybe he doesn't like confined spaces.'

'We have to get out of here.' Alice wrenched the unresponsive door handle. 'We could try shouting for help, I suppose.'

'There's no-one around to hear us. The place is deserted. Everyone's down by the river.'

'There must be an emergency exit somewhere.'

'You see to David while I have a quick look round.'

Mike was back moments later. He pointed up to a skylight.

'That's the only window and it doesn't look like a fire exit to me. It can't have been opened in years.'

Alice sank down on to a convenient bench.

'What I don't understand is who slammed the door?'

'Someone had to have been tailing us.'

'First the gym, now this. It's beginning to spook me and what would be their motivation?'

'Perhaps, like us, they were looking for the box, and David showed them where it was,' Mike supplied the answer.

'If it's the same person who attacked us both times then he or she has got the key, so why didn't they open the locker?'

'Because they heard David saying he couldn't recall Claud's locker number.'

'That only leaves Netta,' Alice said. 'She would know it.'

'And they wouldn't want us getting to Netta first.'

'So they've locked us in here while they go and get the number from her.'

'It makes sense, doesn't it?' Mike looked at Alice.

'If it does then Netta is in serious

danger. She won't be able to scare them away a second time.'

Alice jumped to her feet. David moaned and fell forward.

'We have to get David out of here.'

She knelt down beside him and propped him up against the wall, gently rubbing his back in a gesture of reassurance.

'We will,' Mike said, 'if we can get the wretched door open.'

'You heard David, it's locked from the other side.'

'Then it's got to be the skylight.'

Mike dragged a chair across the floor and positioned it under the window. The chair creaked as he tested its weight.

'Let me,' Alice volunteered.

'You're not going up there.' Mike pulled her back.

'Too late.' Alice wriggled free from his grasp, kicked off her shoes and jumped on to the seat. She stretched her arms up as high as they would go and struggled for the latch. 'I can't reach.' She screwed up her face in frustration.

'Take another look at David and I'll see what I can do.'

'David?' Alice spoke in a gentle voice, anxious not to alarm him. His eyes were still closed and his face ashen. 'Can you hear me?'

He grasped Alice's hand in a firm grip.

'I am weak,' he murmured. 'I am so sorry.'

'You've nothing to apologise for.'

'I have tried counselling.' He squeezed Alice's fingers. 'As a child I was punished by an elder for a trifling misdeed. He locked me in a cupboard. Ever since I fear confined spaces.'

'Mike and I are with you and we'll get you out of here very soon now.'

Alice did her best to comfort David while Mike tried to reach the catch on the window. She watched the chair wobble under him.

'Please, Alice,' the colour was returning to David's face, 'I would like some water. There is a basin in the corner of the room.'

'I'll see what I can do.'

'Thank you,' David released his hold on her hand and patted it gently, 'that would be very nice.'

The tap was stiff and groaned in protest but a few moments later water splashed out of its spout.

'Success,' she called out, 'now all we need is a glass.'

'What's that over there?' Mike, who was still standing on his chair, pointed to a far wall.

'It's a cupboard.'

'What's propped up against it on the far side?'

Alice peered into the dingy corner.

'It's a stick of some sort. No it's not,' she corrected herself, 'it's a hook on a pole.' She snatched it up in delight. 'This is our exit visa.'

'Give it over.' Mike held out a hand.

'Careful,' Alice cautioned. 'That chair doesn't look as though it can hold your weight for much longer.'

'I wish to help,' David volunteered, having drunk some water directly from the tap. 'I feel refreshed now I know we have an escape plan. I will keep hold of the chair.'

Alice bit her lip, not wanting to dampen David's optimism but in her opinion they still were a long way from break out.

'How's it going?' she called up to Mike.

'I've got the hook in the latch, but the window won't budge.'

'It has not been opened in many years,' David said.

'Give it another push,' Alice called up.

Mike grunted then admitted defeat.

'It's no good.'

'Any other suggestions, anyone?' Alice asked.

'Don't let go of the chair, David,' Mike instructed him. 'I'm going to try to climb on to the cupboard.'

'Give me the pole.' Alice held it as Mike grasped the beading at the top of the cupboard.

'I hope this thing won't topple over.'

'Alice, hold the chair. I will steady the cupboard with my weight,' David announced and showing a nimble agility for a man of his years launched his body against the front of the cupboard.

'Right, here we go.' Mike heaved himself up and on to the flat top of the cupboard. 'There must be several years' worth of dust up here.' He coughed then sneezed violently.

'Please,' David implored. 'Remember your health. Violent sneezing is not good for you.'

'Pass over the pole and I'll give it another go.'

Alice swung it across.

'I can feel it beginning to give,' Mike announced.

After several attempts the window surrendered to Mike's pressure and with an agonising creak inched open a fraction letting in a shaft of sunlight and a cooling draught of air.

'Phew.' Mike dusted himself down. 'That mountaineering course Jack and I did two years ago finally paid off.'

'Well done,' David congratulated him.

'Now what do we do?' Alice demanded. 'You'll never wriggle through that gap.'

'Do you think if I got down off this thing you could stand on my shoulders and hoist yourself through?' Mike asked Alice then shook his head. 'Bad idea. Between us we'd probably break the chair.'

'I can do it,' Alice smiled encouragingly at David's stricken face. 'If you and David help me I'll be out of the window and banging on the door to let you out in no time at all.'

Glad she had changed out of her dress in the first aid tent, Alice managed with some skilful manoeuvring to plant her feet on Mike's shoulders and heave herself up towards the goal of the skylight.

'Ugh.' She shook her head as a spider dropped off its cobweb and into her hair.

'Stop moving your feet about or

you'll have us over,' Mike complained.

'I'm doing my best.' Alice grasped the ledge of the window and heaved herself off Mike's shoulders.

'You are doing well,' David shouted encouragement.

'Here goes,' Alice called out, lodging her elbows on the rim of the skylight.

Without the support of Mike's shoulders under her feet Alice fought down her rising panic. Failure was not an option. Netta was in danger and David was threatening to have an all out panic attack.

Breathing heavily she squeezed the upper half of her body through the limited available space. Half in and half out she saw to her relief that the roof was flat.

'You OK?' Mike demanded.

'See you in five. I'm going over the top.' Feeling like an intrepid explorer, Alice wriggled free.

'May the blessings of your ancestors guide you,' David called up.

Alice hid a wry smile. She wasn't

sure what her father Ken would make of her antics but of one thing she was sure he would be right behind her.

'Go for it, girl,' had been one of his sayings, and right now that was exactly what she needed to do.

Crawling around on her knees, she tested the surface carefully. The roofing felt was torn in places and overall did not look very substantial. In the distance Alice could hear revellers on the river. They were making far too much noise to hear her shouts or respond to any calls for help. There wasn't so much as a dog walker around.

She grimaced as her knee scraped against something hard. Feeling around with her hands, she identified it as a railing that appeared to lead to the edge of the roof. Crawling along like a crab she followed its direction and a few moments later leaned over the guttering. An emergency ladder was fixed to the side of the wall.

Biting back the urge to run back and tell Mike and David of her find she swung her foot over and commenced her descent, carefully testing each rung before trusting it with the full force of her weight.

She finally reached the ground and sagged against the ladder, the rungs cold against her forehead. The church clock struck three. The whole adventure had taken less than half an hour, yet it had seemed like five years.

Expelling a lungful of air she straightened up then shrieked as a pair of strong arms gripped her around the waist.

No Time to Lose

'Got you.' Her attacker's breath was warm against her ear. Alice struggled but was unable to break his hold.

'Let go of me.'

She tried elbowing him in the ribs but he was too powerful for her.

'Stop fighting,' he cautioned with a low laugh.

'I'm not scared of you.'

'Then why are you trembling?'

'Because I'm furious.'

Alice fought down a feeling of rising sickness. At the eleventh hour she had failed.

'That sounds like my Alice.'

Her heart was beating so loudly she could barely think straight.

'Your Alice?' she managed to gasp. On trembling legs she spun round to face him. 'Jack?' She had to be imagining things.

'Before your very eyes.'

The late afternoon sun created a halo of light around his head and with his suntanned features he reminded Alice of a Greek god.

'What are you doing here?'

'It's a long story. More to the point, what are you doing shinning down a ladder?'

'Mike and David . . . ' She grabbed Jack's arm. 'We have to rescue them.'

'Intrigue! This gets better and better.' Jack grinned. 'The delights of cruising around the Caribbean begin to wear off after a while. There's only so much fresh fruit you can eat before you start longing for a good old fry up.' He paused. 'Er . . . who's David?'

'David Liu.' Alice gave him a hefty shove.

'Hey, watch what you're doing.'

'Never mind all that now. The door to the locker room closed in on us and we were trapped inside with no way out. I had to escape through the skylight. Come on. We've no time to lose.'

'I'm right with you.' Jack sprang into action. 'Where are we going?'

'Back inside.'

'Glad to see you haven't lost your spirit of adventure.' Jack grinned.

Having him by her side boosted Alice's confidence.

'This is all your fault anyway.' To ease her conscience at her pleasure of seeing him again, Alice decided not to go easy on Jack.

'What did I do?' he protested.

'We wouldn't be in this fix if it hadn't been for you running away and leaving me in the lurch.'

'I'm really sorry, Lallie.' His use of her pet name caused Alice to falter. 'But I'm in a position to make everything up to you. That's why I came looking for you.'

'All I can say to you,' Alice retorted as they jogged along, 'is jade turtles.'

'What was that?'

'Come on. There'll be plenty of time to talk later.'

Alice dragged Jack through the main

entrance and down the darkened corridors.

'Are you sure you know where you're going?' Jack demanded. 'There's a funny smell about the place.'

He wrinkled his nose then sneezed.

'Don't do that. It's bad for your karma.'

'Think I'm coming down with a cold — the change in temperature and all that.'

'This is no time to wimp out.'

'Have you ever known me do that?' Jack demanded.

'No,' Alice was forced to admit.

'Then stop making ridiculous remarks and keep going.'

'We're here.' They came to a halt by the locker room.

Jack inspected the sturdy door with a frown of concentration.

'Is this what all the fuss is about?'

'We're back,' Alice bellowed, grasping the handle. It didn't budge.

'Mike's locked inside here?' Jack hissed at her.

'Alice?' Mike sounded relieved. 'You've been gone hours.'

'There's a security keypad,' Jack who had been inspecting the door murmured in her ear. 'Any idea of the code?'

'Who's that with you?' Mike demanded.

'Your baby brother,' Jack called out. 'I've come to rescue you. Trouble is we're in a bit of a fix out here. The door won't give. We need a code number to get in.'

'Whatever, you're going to have to do something quickly. David's had another turn.'

'This David,' Jack turned to Alice, 'gen me up on him.'

'He's claustrophobic,' Alice explained.

'How did you get out?' Jack asked Alice.

'Through the skylight.'

'Couldn't they get out the same way?'

'David's over sixty and,' Alice shook her head, 'no. We have to get this door open before Lan comes back. I've a suspicion she's behind all this.'

'Lan Nguyen?' Jack's lip curled in disgust at the mention of her name.

'Of course, you know her, don't you?'

Jack shuddered.

'What I think about her is too delicate for a lady's ears.'

'Stop talking sexist nonsense and try to come up with something really useful.'

'How about this — does your friend David know the number to get us in?'

'Mike!' Alice hammered on the door. 'Are you still there?'

'Of course I'm still here,' he snapped, 'and I heard what Jack said but David's in another of his trances.'

'It's what he does.' Alice forestalled the question hovering on Jack's lips.

'If you say so.' He sighed. 'Any chance of nudging him awake, bro?'

'He's out for the count, I fear.'

'Right, then can anyone make an educated guess?'

'How about trying Claud's locker number?'

'You know I am getting seriously confused,' Jack complained. 'Who is Claud?'

'I thought you'd done your home-work on the jade turtle.'

'Stop squabbling, you two,' Mike called out, 'we have an emergency on our hands.'

'Then get that locker number off your transcendental friend.'

'He doesn't know it,' Alice said. 'That's why we were locked up in the first place.'

'I am going to have to ask for footnotes here,' Jack complained.

'Try calling Netta,' Mike shouted.

'She's nothing to do with the Tao centre. She wouldn't set a security number.'

'Just call her,' Mike shouted back.

Alice looked round.

'Where's the telephone?'

'No idea. Haven't you got a mobile?'

'I dropped it in the mud outside the emergency tent and Mike lost his when he fell off the punt into the water.'

'You do seem to have been having an exciting time of things lately.'

Alice spotted a phone on the wall further down the corridor.

'I've got a line,' Alice yanked the telephone off the wall then groaned.

'Problem?' Jack queried.

'I don't know Netta's telephone number. I keyed it into my phone contacts.'

'And your mobile isn't working because you were taking a mud bath. See, I was paying attention,' Jack said.

'Don't you have a mobile?'

'Sorry,' Jack apologised, 'my father-in-law took my old one off me. I meant to replace it but when you're in the Caribbean you've got other things on your mind.'

'Hey!' A shout from the other side of the door made them both jump.

'Are you OK, bro?' Jack asked with a note of panic.

'Would you believe it? David had a mobile on him all the time. It's fallen out of the pocket in his sleeve.'

'You mean all that climbing out of skylights was unnecessary?' Jack demanded.

'There's no signal in here but,' he paused, 'I do have Netta's landline number.'

'Don't keep us in suspense,' Jack ordered. 'Lallie's standing by at the ready.'

'Her name's Alice,' Mike said in a cold voice.

'We'll argue about that later,' Jack replied. 'Number, please.'

'There's no reply.' Alice screwed up her face in disbelief, fighting down a sob of frustration as no-one answered her call.

'What was that number again?' Jack called out to Mike.

'If she's not answering, what's the point?'

'Give it to me,' Jack bellowed.

Mike repeated it patiently while Jack scribbled it down on a scrap of paper.

'Try the last four numbers on the keypad,' he instructed Alice.

'Do you think it will work?'

'Can you come up with any other suggestions?'

'No luck.'

'The first four?'

'No.' Alice shook her head.

'Try the middle four.' Jack began to look downhearted.

'It's not going to work.'

'Are you sure David set it in the first place? I mean it could have been someone else.'

'Then we'll never get it right.'

'Hey, never admit defeat.' Jack straightened his shoulders. 'There must be something we aren't doing.'

'Have you pressed enter?' Mike called out from the other side of the door.

'Why didn't I think of that?' Jack smacked his forehead with the open palm of his hand. 'Start again, Alice,' he said emphasising her name.

'The last four numbers don't work. It'll have to be the first four.'

'This is getting tedious,' Jack complained.

As Alice pressed the enter button a green light flashed, the keypad made a mechanical noise and the door swung open.

'Before we do anything else, lodge the wretched thing open with a chair or something,' Jack said, taking charge of the situation.

'Jack.'

Mike greeted his brother with open arms. Alice looked away as the brothers embraced.

'Hey, what's with the lump on your forehead? I can't leave you alone for five minutes, can I?' Jack punched Mike playfully on the shoulder.

'At least I don't desert my post or leave a female in distress.'

'Alice doesn't do that.' Jack made a gesture with his hands. 'The female in distress thing.'

'Too right she doesn't. Do you know it was Alice who was responsible for this?' He indicated his forehead.

'Nothing would surprise me when it comes to Alice.'

The brothers grinned and punched each other again.

'When you two have finished bonding, can we please get David to his feet?' Alice was bending over his huddled form.

'Breath of fresh air is what's needed here.' Jack slung one of David's arms around his neck. 'Easy does it. Think you can move your legs?'

David murmured something.

'Didn't quite catch that. I'm Jack, by the way, but we'll save the introductions for later, shall we?'

With Mike supporting David's other arm the trio staggered out of the locker room.

'Look, there's the fire exit.' Alice pointed to a green sign on the wall. 'Let's use that.'

'What if we set off the alarms?' Mike demanded.

'That right now is the least of our worries. Lead the way, Lal — I mean Alice.'

Alice pushed down the heavy security

bar and the door yielded.

'No alarms, thank goodness. Deep breathing, everyone,' Jack said as they staggered on to the grass.

'There's a bench over there,' Mike said. 'Do you think you could help me lug it across? David doesn't look too comfortable on the ground. Alice?'

'I'll do it if you keep an eye on David,' Jack volunteered and began shunting the bench across the grass. 'This thing is heavier than it looks.

'Any suggestions as to what we do now?' Jack asked as he sat down on the bench and crossed his arms. 'I don't know about anyone else but I am not going back in there ever. How's it going with David?'

'He's coming round,' Alice replied.

'Good — because we need a serious catch up.'

'David? You're safe now. Can you sit on the bench while you recover?'

'I have been such a nuisance,' he gasped out.

'Not at all.' Jack leaped to his feet.

'Here, let me help you.'

'You, my dear friend,' the twinkle was back in David's eye as the colour returned to his cheeks, 'have to be a rooster.'

'Are you sure he's feeling better?' Jack turned to Alice. 'He called me a chicken.'

'Not a chicken, a rooster,' David said. 'They are brave and resilient.'

'Now that does sound like me.' Jack puffed out his chest.

'But they can also be self absorbed and pretentious.'

'That also sounds like you,' Alice agreed. Jack made a face.

'And I thought David was my new best friend.'

The sound of a twig cracking behind them made Alice jump.

'Nobody moves,' a cold voice instructed.

Nightmare Scenario

'Christine.' Alice took a hesitant step towards her.

'Stay where you are,' Christine insisted. 'And you.' She nodded at Jack.

'Where's Mike?' Alice hissed at him.

Jack glanced over her shoulder.

'Not sure,' he admitted. 'Look, Lallie, I'm having difficulty keeping up with all this. Who's the female with the sludgy green hair?'

'The dark red tips indicate malice and anger.' David was twitching with agitation.

Jack looked more confused than ever.

'What is going on?' he pleaded.

'I know it sounds silly,' Alice confided to Christine, 'but I think the colour of your hair is scaring David.'

She moved between them, hoping David would calm down if Christine were out of his eye line.

'You do not seem to understand the seriousness of the situation.' David gave Alice a sharp nudge in the back that almost caused her to topple over. She stifled a shriek of surprise.

'Take it easy, my friend.' Jack patted David on the shoulder. 'You're in the fresh air now. There's no need to panic or start pushing people out of the way. Remember, deep breaths.'

'I don't think that's going to work.' Alice looked worried. 'I've never known him so stressed.'

'There's nothing to worry about,' Jack insisted, still trying to calm him down.

'Netta.' David circled his fingers around Jack's arm causing him to wince. 'She is in trouble.'

'Thank goodness you're here, Christine.' Alice turned back to face her. 'We think Lan Nguyen might be holding Netta hostage.'

'She is.' Christine's eyes narrowed. 'And I said don't move.'

Alice's smile faltered.

'Don't worry, David won't attack you. I'm sure it was a one off.'

'At a rough guess,' Jack butted in, 'I'd say your friend Christine is attempting to hold us hostage, too.'

'What are you talking about?' Alice demanded.

'Haven't you noticed that thing she is brandishing at us?'

'It's a warrior sword,' David said in a faint voice as Christine raised it in an aggressive stance. 'It hangs on the wall of the Tao centre.'

'And which I had the foresight to grab up as a precaution,' Christine added. 'It rather puts me in charge of the situation — no? I warn you, I won't hesitate to use it. It's heavier than a fencing foil but I can cope.'

The blade glinted in the sunlight.

'What's the matter with everyone?' Alice protested. 'There's no need to go all mediaeval on us, Christine. We're friends, aren't we?'

'She doesn't look all that friendly to me,' Jack said.

'She is Netta's granddaughter.'

'I told you before,' Christine said in an ice-cold voice, 'Netta was my grandfather's second wife. She is no relation to me.'

'Has everybody had a personality transplant today?' Alice demanded.

'I don't think so,' Jack spoke in a calm voice.

'Then why are Christine and David acting out of character?'

'Are they?' Jack sounded unconvinced.

Alice turned away from him in disgust.

'Look, Christine, put the sword down, it's unsettling David.'

'Since when did you give me orders?'

'I don't, I mean . . . ' Alice lapsed into silence as words failed her.

'I think you're wasting your breath,' Jack cautioned.

Christine brandished the blade with a menacing flick of her wrist.

'You appear to be the brains of the outfit.' Her aquamarine eyes narrowed as she surveyed the group in front of her. 'May I know who was responsible for your break out?'

'That was Alice. I'm Jack,' he introduced himself. 'I don't believe we've met.'

'I don't believe we have.'

'It was you who locked us in, wasn't it?' Alice demanded, losing patience with Christine, 'and it was you who attacked me in the fitness centre, wasn't it?'

'It was child's play ripping the key from your neck while you were fumbling around in the dark.' Christine couldn't resist gloating.

'Why have you been stalking us?'

'Stop wasting time,' Christine snapped. 'We need to get down to business.'

'If Lan Nguyen is holding Netta hostage,' Jack spoke slowly.

'She is,' Christine affirmed.

'Then you are in charge of the situation here, aren't you?' Jack replied.

'I have always been in charge.' There was a sharper edge to Christine's voice.

'You will also know we will do anything to help you because we don't want Netta hurt,' Alice said.

'Absolutely correct.'

'If anything happens to Netta . . . ' David's voice rose in alarm.

'You'll do what?' Christine taunted. 'Forsake your pacifist principles? I do not think so.'

'But why are you doing all this?' Alice demanded.

'It is not obvious?'

'Not to me,' Alice replied in an equally cold voice.

'When Netta came on the scene it was as if my grandfather lost his head.' Christine made a gesture of annoyance. 'Before that I had been his little demoiselle.

'He would buy me presents, take me places and give me pocket money. I would have a good time with him. After Netta lured him away from me these treats stopped.'

'It's time you grew up,' Alice said in anger. 'When my father remarried I

206

didn't act like a spoiled brat. I was pleased for him. You should have been pleased that Claud found happiness with Netta.'

'The turtle should have been mine.'

'The turtle was an anniversary present from Claud to Netta.'

'What use is a valuable objet d'art like that to Netta? She keeps it hidden away in a box and never shows it to anyone. She does not care for these things. She does not even respect my grandfather's memory.'

'That's nonsense,' Alice protested.

'She prefers the company of this,' Christine glared at David, 'sage. So, the turtle is mine,' she insisted. 'I am faithful to my grandfather.'

'Don't argue with her,' Jack cautioned Alice. 'Give her the wretched turtle and let's get out of here. It's not worth getting sliced in two.'

'We can't.'

'Can't what?'

'Give her the turtle.'

'Why not?'

'It's gone missing.'

'What?'

'It disappeared from its showcase.'

'Why didn't you tell me that earlier?' Jack's look of anger was matched by Alice's sense of outrage.

'It can't have slipped your mind that you've been cruising the Caribbean on your honeymoon. Funnily enough you didn't leave a forwarding address and to refresh your memory, your father-in-law blocked all calls. So how exactly was I supposed to get in touch with you?'

Jack had the grace to look shame-faced.

'We wouldn't have suited, Lallie, and I'm sorry.'

'Sorry doesn't even begin to cover it.'

David, who had perched on a wooden seat, rose slowly to his feet.

'I have the turtle,' he announced.

Jack and Alice fell silent, their eyes swivelling in his direction.

'David,' Alice took a concerned step towards him, 'you're not yourself. You're confused.'

He drew himself up to his full height.

'I stole the turtle.'

'Why?'

'That's easy. When Netta turned him down, he stole her turtle to get back at her? I'm right, aren't I?' Christine sneered.

'You are wrong,' David replied with calm dignity.

'Pah!' Christine gave a disbelieving snort of disgust.

'I knew Lan Nguyen had her eye on it and I suspected she would stop at nothing to get it. I persuaded Netta to let us display it at the festival then I took it from its display cabinet when everyone was at the yellow party.'

'To save Netta from harm? How very touching.' Christine's lip curled in disbelief. 'Well you'd better go and get it, hadn't you?'

'What if he doesn't want to?' Alice challenged.

'Then he'll regret it.'

'You can't threaten us, we are four against one.'

Alice grimaced as Jack trod on her foot.

'She means three,' Jack said in a loud voice, drowning Alice's protest.

'Whatever.' Christine appeared to lose interest. 'Let me spell things out for you. If Lan does not hear from me within the hour Netta will suffer the consequences.' David gave a small moan of distress. 'You don't want that on your conscience, do you?'

'Please,' David pleaded, 'do not harm her.'

'I won't if you do as you're told.'

The sounds of increased revelry drifted up from the water. How could this nightmare be happening so close to normal everyday life, Alice thought? Surely someone would come looking for them. Had Mike gone for help? If so, it was important to distract Christine.

'You don't need the money, Christine.' She played for time. 'You have a wonderful job.'

'I had a wonderful job.'

'Travelling the world.'

'My skills are, how do you say, surplus to requirements? There was a downturn in the company's fortune.' Christine scowled. 'It was necessary to make cutbacks. I was a victim of these cutbacks so I thought my grandfather would have wanted to help me out. The turtle was doing nothing in its wooden box. When Alice did not deliver, Lan approached me with a view to doing a deal.'

'I congratulate you.'

Alice clenched her fists as Jack smiled at Christine. It was a smile she knew so well. He was going to change sides. Alice's protest died as, on the pretence of putting his arm around her, Jack dug his fingers into the soft flesh around her waist and delivered a sharp nip.

'With the turtle and the contents of Claud's security box,' Christine continued crowing over them, 'Lan and I will have all we need to make a sale to Selwyn Bishop.'

'And when he discovers the turtle is a fake?'

'I will destroy Claud's evidence. Should Selwyn Bishop suspect anything it will be too late. The deal will have been struck. Come, no more wasting time. David, the turtle.'

'I left my keys in the locker room.' He made a gesture of obeisance, lowering his eyes to the ground.

'He can't go back inside,' Alice protested.

'David has a problem with confined spaces.'

'Then he will have to man up and deal with it.' Christine gestured with her sword.

'Best do as she says,' Jack murmured in Alice's ear.

The chair was where it had been left lodged against the door. Alice could feel David's body shaking.

'It's all right — you can stay outside,' she soothed him. 'Tell me where your keys are and I will get them.'

'I'll get them.' Christine dangled

Claud's locker key in front of Alice. 'You open Claud's security box. It is on the far right, at the end of the middle row.'

Making sure David was comfortably seated on a spare chair in the doorway Alice knelt down and inserted the key.

'It doesn't work.' Alice tried to turn the key.

'Of course it works,' Christine insisted. 'I have the number here in Claud's handwriting.'

'Looks like we've got the wrong key,' Jack said.

'Or the wrong locker,' Alice suggested.

There was a disturbance in the doorway.

'Look out,' Jack shouted.

'What's wrong?' Christine demanded.

'David's collapsed.'

'He's faking it. Get up,' Christine ordered.

In one swift movement Jack pushed her to one side, grabbed Alice by the wrist and pulled her out of the locker room. David leaped to his feet and pulled the chair away allowing the door to slam to behind them. For a moment no-one moved.

'I am a good actor, am I not?' It was David who spoke first as he looked to Alice and Jack for approval.

'David, that was brilliant.' Alice flung her arms around him.

Jack dusted himself down.

'With Christine safely locked up shall we go see what's happened to Mike?' he enquired in a calm voice.

To the Rescue

Mike crouched behind a shrub. Through an open window he could hear raised voices coming from the direction of the farmhouse.

Abandoning his car behind a pile of rusty machinery at the top of the drive he had sped down the incline on tiptoe, careful not to make too much noise, but now he hesitated.

Whoever the female with green hair outside the Tao centre had been, instinct told him from the expression on her face and the way she handled her sword that she meant business. It was a ridiculous situation to be in and if he hadn't seen it with his own eyes Mike would not have believed it was real.

He hadn't wanted to abandon Alice but he knew Jack would look out for her, so while no-one was looking he had seized his chance and slipped away.

Now scuttling across the drive on all fours, Mike headed for Netta's tumble-down outhouse. It had an abandoned air of neglect that would provide perfect cover for Mike while he thought things through.

Careful to avoid discarded flowerpots and a broken garden rake he crawled under the surrounding wooden fence. A shout caused him to freeze and duck down again. He gritted his teeth and held his breath.

Had he been spotted? In a knee jerk reaction his foot kicked out at some-thing solid. Grimacing, he lunged for the obstacle and snatched it up before it toppled over and gave away his cover.

Stilling his breath he listened out for the sound of pounding feet. With his heart beating rapidly, he peered through a gap in some planking.

Everywhere was eerily quiet. The only sound now was the breeze rustling through the long grass. His fingers tightened around the base of the wooden pole he was clutching. He bit down a cry of triumph as he realised it was the butt of Netta's fake firearm. In the cold light of day he could see it was realistic enough to fool someone into thinking it was real.

Mike hesitated. It had worked before. Could he pull off the same stunt again? Netta would know the gun was a fake but she was hardly likely to expose him.

Screwing up his eyes, Mike tried to recall the layout of the interior of the farmhouse. He wished he knew where everyone was and whether Lan had a weapon and indeed if it was her holding Netta hostage, but who else could it be? And who else was there with her besides Netta?

He stiffened at the sound of more raised voices. Things were turning ugly. There was no time to lose. Easing into an upright position he hoisted his wooden weapon into the air and with the advantage of surprise on his side strode towards the farmhouse.

Alice released hold of a beaming David.

'You are the business.' She did a dance of delight.

'Mike?' Jack prompted when neither of them took any notice of him. 'Any idea where my brother might have gone?' He raised his voice. 'Alice, listen up. This is important.'

'What? Mike? Right, um, to see Netta?' she suggested.

'And we have to get out there — now,' David urged Jack. He was no longer smiling.

'Shouldn't we check the centre first?'

'Why?' Alice demanded.

'He may be hiding away somewhere, you know — waiting for his big moment?'

Jack's voice tailed away as he took in the expression on Alice face.

'Unlike some,' she said in a cold voice, 'Mike does not show off.'

'Now hang on a moment,' Jack protested. 'I wasn't suggesting anything of the sort.'

'Then exactly what were you hinting at?'

'You have a car?' David interrupted before Jack could reply.

'I hired one.'

'Good. Where did you leave it?'

'Down by the river.'

'Then let's go,' David assumed charge.

'What about Christine?' Jack asked. 'Shouldn't we do something about her, I mean, we've locked her away.'

'She'll come to no harm where she is for the moment and it will do her good to have a taste of her own medicine.'

'What happened to your pacifist principles?' Jack raised an eyebrow at David.

'And supposing she gets panic attacks?' Alice was also experiencing a twinge of conscience.

David nodded.

'I'll contact the janitor, Dawson. He won't stir himself immediately. He never does. The delay should give us time to get out to the farmhouse. Now hurry — there is no time to lose.'

'David seems keen on this Netta. Is there anything going on I should know about?' Jack demanded as he led the way to his car.

'They go way back,' Alice panted as she tried to keep up with his long strides.

'Like that, is it?' Jack raised his eyebrows.

'And unlike some he doesn't desert his friends.'

'Can we do the blame thing later?' Jack asked. 'Here's my car.'

David caught them up.

'Dawson was not best pleased at being called out but he did not ask awkward questions. I will sit in the back. Please let us drive swiftly, I do not want further delay.'

'Are things really this urgent?' Jack murmured to Alice as he turned the ignition key.

'I don't think you realise how ruthless Lan can be.'

'I know how tricky she can be,' he admitted.

'Step on it, please,' David pleaded.

Jack gunned the engine into life.

'If you're right and anything's happened to Mike that woman will pay the price.'

★   ★   ★

'That's Mike's car.' Alice pointed to where it had been abandoned at the top of Netta's drive.

'Well, I'm not hiding away behind any pile of old junk. I am driving right up to the front door,' Jack announced. 'I'm having none of this undercover lark.'

'Go, go,' David urged from the back seat.

'Steady,' Jack cautioned as David bounced from side to side in agitation. 'There's no need to wreck the suspension.'

David continued to mutter under his breath as Jack turned off the ignition.

'What are you doing?' Alice demanded.

'We'll freewheel the rest of the way.

Don't want to cause unnecessary panic.'

'Careful how you go,' Alice cautioned as Jack steered noiselessly down the drive, 'Mind the potholes.'

'I think I'm going to have trouble with the damage waiver clause,' he announced, as there was a bump followed by an unpleasant scraping sound from under the floor panel. 'Hasn't Netta heard of tarmac?'

'Look,' David pointed a finger towards the conservatory at the side of the house.

'Where?' Jack demanded.

'There, that's Netta and there's someone with her.' He squinted. 'I can't see what they are doing.'

Jack swerved to the right and brought the car to an abrupt halt.

'Everybody out,' he ordered.

David was running towards the farmhouse before Alice had even opened her door.

'Wait for me,' she called out. 'Go after him, Jack,' she shouted. 'He's more frail than he looks.'

'I'm here, Netta,' David called out as he reached the conservatory door.

Jack yanked him back almost pulling them both down.

'For goodness' sake,' he yelled. 'This was supposed to be a covert operation. You'll ruin everything.'

Alice lost her balance as she collided with them in the doorway. If it hadn't been for Jack's steadying hand, the three of them would have landed in a heap on the ground.

'Well done, guys,' Jack said with a disgusted look on his face, 'our cover's blown. Any suggestions as to what we do now?'

David performed a deep bow.

'That wasn't quite what I had in mind,' Jack said, a trace of sarcasm in his voice.

'Glad you could make it. What took you so long?' a calm voice enquired behind them.

Alice spun round and was confronted by a pair of amused deep blue eyes.

All is Revealed

The yellow morning sun streaming through the primrose blinds of Netta's kitchen window clashed hideously with her vivid orange top. With managing director authority she presided over the head of the scrubbed pine table, her eyes alight with excitement.

'I've been in some tight spots in my time.' The corners of her eyes creased into amusement. 'But I tell you this one was up there with the best.' Her smile widened. 'I miss those days when you never knew what was around the next corner. But where are my manners?' She addressed the small group seated around the table. 'I hope you all had a good night's sleep?'

There was a general murmur of assent.

'Good. David,' she snapped her

fingers, 'the percolator. Our guests need some coffee.'

'I would prefer jasmine tea,' he said in a quiet voice.

'If you must.' Netta sighed. 'You know where everything is. There's orange juice too and if anybody wants toast I think there's some bread about the place somewhere.'

David winked at Alice and rose to his feet.

'We have some serious catching up to do,' Netta insisted. 'I would like updates from you all.'

'That Lan Nguyen really took me in good and proper.' Selwyn Bishop was the first to speak.

'You're not the only one,' Jack agreed with a rueful smile.

'I thought when she arranged the meeting here with Ms McKenzie that the sale of the jade turtle was a done deal.'

'And it was only when you got here you realised you had been duped?' Mike said.

'Exactly — and I can't thank you enough,' Selwyn shook him warmly by the hand, 'for saving the day.'

'Mike is my hero, too,' Netta butted in.

'What about me?' Jack protested, managing to look effortlessly laid back after spending the night on Mike's camp bed.

Alice squeezed Mike's hand, a gesture not unnoticed by Jack.

'If it hadn't been for Mike, goodness knows what would have happened.'

'I am in everyone's debt.'

Alice ignored Selwyn's contribution.

'Mike was there for me after you left me in the lurch,' she said, her hazel eyes pinned on Jack.

'Thanks, Alice, but when it comes to dealing with my brother I can give a good account of myself,' Mike cautioned.

'You don't have to give an account of anything, big brother.' Jack slapped him on the shoulder. 'You're one of the good guys.'

'I would like an account of everything,' Netta insisted. 'After I was bundled off to bed by that child of a doctor I missed all the fun.'

'You were in shock.' David bustled around behind her. 'You needed a good night's sleep.'

'Maybe I did,' Netta conceded, 'but now I am back to my old self I want to know exactly what happened.'

'One thing at a time,' David said mildly.

'Well, don't hang about. Those two,' she nodded to Jack and Alice, 'look like they might come to blows.'

'Sorry.' Alice uttered a shamefaced apology as Mike leaned forward and took firm hold of Alice's hand.

'You've every right to be angry with Jack and you have my full permission to make him pay for all the trouble he's caused but let's leave it for later.'

'Hang about,' Jack protested. 'I didn't have to come back, you know.'

'What do you mean you didn't have to come back?' Alice was close to boiling point. 'Where's your sense of honour?'

'Later,' Mike insisted.

'As hostess, why don't you go first, Ms McKenzie?' It was Selwyn who again rescued the situation.

'It's Netta,' she said before sitting back in her chair, 'and it's difficult to know where to start, really. As you all probably suspected, my turtle is a fake.'

'A mock turtle?' Jack's grin died out as no-one smiled at his joke.

'Claud discovered evidence verifying that the gold decoration on my turtle came from a mine not discovered at the time of the original supposed commission. He also discovered that the gold used was of a different origin to the jade.'

'I suspected something like that,' Selwyn admitted, 'but it was a case of my heart ruling my head. I wanted to believe the turtle was the real thing and Lan Nguyen talks a good game.'

'It was the same with me and Christine,' Netta added in a quiet voice.

'I wanted her to be a part of our lives but deep down I sensed she was a troubled individual.'

David put out a hand to comfort her. Alice feared she might shake him off but she seemed grateful for the gesture.

'I knew she resented me but I never thought she would go as far as she did.'

'I would have given her the wretched turtle if I'd known how much it meant to her, but I thought it meant as much to you,' David said in his quiet voice.

Netta cast him an indulgent smile.

'Is that why you stole it?'

'I merely removed it to a safer place,' he corrected her.

'Why?'

'Because I didn't want anyone hurting you for the sake of a trinket.'

Netta's face softened.

'Its value was only ever sentimental.'

'And how did you get in on the act?' Selwyn turned his attention to Mike.

'When he charged through the door I don't know who was the more shocked.' Netta chuckled.

'I had the advantage of surprise,' Mike explained.

'I nearly exploded with laughter when I saw you waving Old Faithful in the air, but it did the trick.'

'Talking of tricks, you pulled a neat one, David, pretending to faint outside the locker room.' Alice smiled at him.

'I wasn't sure it was going to work,' David admitted, 'or that I could fool Christine.'

'Where is Christine now?' Selwyn asked.

'She and Lan have done a vanishing trick and good riddance to them,' Netta said.

'I can't imagine what the janitor thought or what story Christine told him when he rescued her but he is a lazy individual with not much imagination so I don't think we need worry that anyone will go public,' David explained.

'You're not going to take things further, are you, Netta?' Alice asked.

'That depends on Selwyn.'

'I didn't part with any money so I'd

be pleased to draw a line under the whole affair.'

'That's generous of you,' Jack said.

'If the story got out of how I was fooled by a two-bit conman . . . or do I mean person? Anyway, it would damage my international reputation, so if everyone's in agreement, we say nothing?'

'Agreed.' They all nodded.

Selwyn looked at his watch.

'In fact, if you'll excuse me, I have a plane to catch.'

'What are you after now?' Netta enquired. 'A pyramid or two?'

'Netta, please, respect,' David implored as a distracted Selwyn ducked under the table to look for his briefcase.

'I never let it out of my sight.' He held it up in triumph. 'Nice to have met you all. If you ever come stateside, look me up. I can promise you a warm welcome.'

'He wasn't as bad as people said,' Netta remarked after Selwyn had made his departure.

'And it looks like we've got one satisfied customer,' Jack added.

'Lan was our client, not Selwyn,' Alice replied.

'You know that story she told about me making off with her commission wasn't true. I'm amazed you fell for it, Lallie.'

'You left unpaid bills everywhere,' Mike said in a harsh voice, 'what was Alice supposed to think?'

'I've settled everything,' Jack said. 'Alice is no longer in debt.'

'Where have I heard that story before?'

'This time it's true. Anyway I've got to go as well.'

'Not so fast.' Mike put out a hand to detain his brother.

'Viv will be expecting me.'

'She can wait a little longer and the sooner you tell us how and why you appeared out of nowhere the sooner you can leave,' Mike insisted. 'You owe it to Alice if nothing else. We're waiting,' Mike insisted as Jack cast a smile at Alice.

'Difficult to know where to start, really,' he admitted, 'but Mr Hollingsworth, Viv's father, had to fly home urgently because his mother was taken ill. Of course Viv wanted to be with him so we all came back together.

'Visitors were restricted to close family and as I don't know Viv's grandmother we decided I would come on down to Saltwich to visit Mike and you.' Jack cast another look at Alice.

'Viv agreed to your meeting up with me?' Alice repeated in disbelief.

'She knew I had to put things right between us. Viv's a wonderful girl.' The look on Jack's face told Alice all she needed to know. He was in love with his new wife. 'You'll love her, too, when we all meet up.'

'We are straying off the point,' Mike reminded his brother.

'I don't know what Lan told you exactly but the commission I undertook was to approach Netta to see if she would be interested in parting with her turtle but no money changed hands.'

'Lan told me you were going to steal it for her.'

The colour drained from Jack's face.

'That's not true.'

'Why should I believe you? You disappeared without a trace, leaving a stack of unpaid bills.'

'After I met Viv I wasn't thinking straight. That's the reason I took off without a word. I know I've sailed close to the wind on occasions but I would never steal anything from anybody.'

'I informed you how devious Lan could be,' David said quietly.

'I came back as soon as I could and like I said you're now debt free, Lallie.'

'You paid off all outstanding debts?' Mike demanded.

'I did.'

'How?'

A smile tugged at the corner of Jack's mouth.

'Grandmother's inheritance.'

'The one you squandered? Jack,' there was a note of panic in Mike's voice, 'what have you done?'

'I didn't squander all of it,' Jack protested, looking hurt. 'I invested some in a finance company.' He paused.

'Which like all your ventures failed spectacularly.'

'That's not quite true,' Jack corrected him. 'The company actually got taken over. There was this huge bidding war.'

'You were bought out?' Mike sounded amazed.

Jack nodded with a happy smile.

'Viv agreed I should use the windfall to clear everything up with Lallie. When I arrived here I found her shinning down a ladder.' He shrugged. 'So I thought as there was an adventure going I'd better join in. The rest you know.'

A stunned silence followed Jack's tale.

'Viv must be a really special person,' Alice said in a faint voice.

'She read me the riot act when I confessed how I had treated you. I was left in no doubt that if I didn't make good on the loss,' Jack gave a shamefaced smile, 'well, she threatened to walk out on me.'

'A female walking out on you?' Mike repeated in amazement. 'There's a first.'

'It had preyed on my mind that you deserved better, Lallie,' Jack mumbled. 'If it's any consolation Viv and I are really happy together and I couldn't bear the thought of losing Viv, so I did as she told me. Am I forgiven?'

Alice could feel a warm flush working its way up her neck as she realised her love now for Jack was no more than that of a sister for her brother and she was grateful he had had the sense to realise this.

'There's nothing to forgive,' she said, 'and thanks, Jack, for everything.'

'Can I leave now?' he asked in a plaintive voice. 'I think Selwyn's taxi has arrived. I'm sure he'll give me a lift.' He smiled at Alice and kissed her on the cheek. 'I've never had a sister,' he whispered. 'Don't let Mike down.' Then with a quick 'I'll be in touch' to his brother, he was gone.

'What was all that whispering about?' Mike asked in a suspicious voice.

'I'll tell you later,' Alice said, still trying to control her rapid heartbeat.

'David . . . ' Netta was speaking again.

'Yes?' He started at the sound of her voice.

'You didn't believe that nonsense about there being a curse on the turtle, did you?'

'I took the turtle,' David patiently repeated his story, 'because I was worried for your safety, not because of a silly unfounded story.'

'I told you I could look after myself.'

'Can you?' David raised his voice in the first show of annoyance Alice had seen from him. 'You have been held hostage, almost robbed blind by an ungrateful step granddaughter and caused so much upset to our dear friends here. You are lucky we are all still talking to you.'

'What happened wasn't my fault and

I did offer to help Alice pay off her debts.'

'One thing I don't understand,' Alice interrupted their heated exchange, 'is why the key to Claud's locker didn't work.'

'That is a good question, Alice,' David said, sounding more like his old self.

'And can we expect an answer some time soon?' Netta asked.

'When Netta entrusted me with its safety I sensed bad vibes.'

'More tosh.' Netta pulled a face.

'When Alice told me Christine had been asking about it, I knew my suspicions were correct so I gave you the wrong key. To my shame I have to admit I don't know which of the security boxes it would open. I had no idea Christine would go as far as attacking you for it.'

'And how did you manage to slip away?' Alice looked at Mike.

'There was no way Christine could keep her eye on all of us. I used David's attack as a distraction. Someone had to get to Netta.'

'I am very glad you did, my young dragon.'

'Dragon?' Mike looked perplexed.

'A symbol associated with the male element yang.'

'He does a lot of that sort of stuff,' Netta observed. 'I'm a dog.'

'Lucky, loyal and lovable.'

'That's me,' Netta agreed.

The little group fell silent.

'So, David,' Netta broke the silence, 'I'm sure there's a philosophy somewhere in your archives that says if you save someone's life they are for ever in your debt.'

'You owe me nothing, Netta.' David's cheeks turned pink.

'But you owe me something.'

An uncertain look crossed David's face.

'I do?'

'When are we going to legalise our relationship?'

The Answer is Yes

Guests mingled outside the church. The civil ceremony an hour beforehand had been a private affair after which Netta and David had chosen to invite everyone to a mixed denominational blessing embracing David's Taoist values and Netta's personal beliefs. It had been a moving and dignified occasion.

Everything had been arranged with such surprising haste that even David had been forced to caution Netta.

'Nature does not like to be hurried.'

'No point in hanging around,' Netta insisted. 'Neither of us is getting any younger and we've waited long enough, don't you think?'

After that David had given in to Netta.

'You know what, David?' Alice had caught up with him on a day he had been visiting Netta. 'You are a fraud.'

'I beg your pardon?' he asked, looking hurt.

'I think you are secretly enjoying the excitement your engagement has brought to the centre and the local community.'

'Please,' he implored, 'do not discuss this point of view with Netta. You see, if Netta senses my enthusiasm she will probably cancel her plans and I have waited so long.'

'Your secret is safe with me,' Alice assured him, 'and Netta will go through with the ceremony even if I have to march her down the aisle myself.'

Mike now stood next to Alice as a proud David posed for photographs together with Netta who had chosen to wear a vibrant orange hat and matching silk suit designed by one of David's attendants.

'It looks like Netta has gone for the full chakra bit.' Alice smiled. 'Did you know orange is a sacral healing colour?'

'Not sure I did. To be honest, today

has passed in a blur. Have you ever seen such a sight?'

The area surrounding the church was a sea of peacock colours, fluttering silks coupled with sombre business suits sporting garish ties and an array of media types who looked slightly put out by having their dress code upstaged by the myriad colours sported by David's assistants.

Alice had chosen a classic oatmeal dress and, in response to Netta's request that everyone should wear bright colours, had coupled her outfit with a patchwork jacket.

'Do I look all right?' Mike had asked Alice moments before the start of the ceremony. He did up the top button of his black and white geometric patterned shirt and adjusted his tangerine tie. 'Jack's wedding dress code was a lot more traditional,' he confided.

'You look fine,' Alice assured him. The white lie caused her crossed fingertips to tingle.

'Jack was always the smart one in the

family,' Mike reminisced.

'Stop comparing yourself to Jack.' Alice frowned.

'Talking of chakras,' Mike leaned in towards Alice, 'there are some pretty alternative guests about the place.'

'Netta has led a colourful life and I think it's fun.'

Alice couldn't help noticing how the sun created highlights of gold on Mike's hair as they waited for the photo call to finish and as if sensing the moment Mike turned back to face her.

'You won't go all feminist on me if I say something, will you?' he asked.

'Try me,' Alice said in a careful voice.

'That gold edging on your jacket, I don't know what it is called.'

'Braid.' Alice helped him out.

'That's the stuff.'

'What about it?'

'It makes your eyes look all golden, too.'

Mike looked like a man who feared he may gave gone too far as he lapsed into silence.

'I think,' David, who had approached without either Alice or Mike noticing, put in, 'that my new life will be challenging.' He glanced across to Netta, an indulgent smile on his face. 'But I have known my lovely wife a long time. We will be happy together.'

Recovering her composure, Alice gave him a swift hug.

'That's all that matters and you don't need me to tell you to stand up for yourself,' Alice said. 'You've shown how you can rise to the occasion.'

'When the people I love are threatened, it is a natural reaction,' he said with a modest smile.

'We couldn't be more pleased for the two of you,' Mike added.

'Thank you for your good wishes.' David bowed in his courteous fashion. 'I hope I am not being presumptuous when I say it is my dearest wish and I know Netta would join in my sentiment, that you will both follow our example.' His eyes twinkled mischievously as he backed away. 'Now if you will excuse me?'

'What did he mean by that?' Alice turned to Mike.

'I think it's a reference to commitment,' Mike replied. 'It's quite fashionable at the moment,' he added.

Alice could feel the colour rising in her cheeks. She swiftly changed the subject.

'Talking of commitment, have you heard from Jack?'

'His text said Viv's grandmother is on the mend and Viv has forgiven him for deserting you. He also mentioned that the four of us must get together some time.'

'I doubt that will be possible,' Alice said.

'You're not thinking of moving on, are you?' Mike frowned at her.

'I don't know what my plans are,' Alice admitted.

'You promised to stay,' Mike reminded her.

'I agreed to stay for David and Netta's ceremony but now the service is over I have to think about my future.'

'We should both be grateful to Jack,' Mike said.

'Not that again.' Alice raised her eyes in frustration.

'I know he behaved badly but he had the courage to leave a relationship that wasn't working.'

'I thought it was,' Alice said stubbornly.

'Jack didn't.'

'Then he could have told me to my face instead of running away.'

'Can you honestly say you still miss him?'

It was a question Alice couldn't answer.

'How did you feel when he came back into your life?' Mike persisted.

'Look, can we talk about something else?' Alice demanded.

'I need to know,' Mike answered with mulish obstinacy.

'Why?'

'Venetia tells me you haven't been in

touch with her,' he said, changing the subject.

'Should I have been?'

'You promised to make an appointment with her to discuss her proposal regarding the agency.'

'I promised no such thing,' Alice was adamant. 'You suggested I contact her but I made no commitment.'

'There's that word again.' Mike smiled.

'Don't joke, Mike, this is serious.'

'Then please, Alice, contact Venetia.'

'Why? You told me that you and she had come up with a plan to keep the agency going if you stepped into Jack's shoes.'

'That about sums it up but you need Venetia to spell things out properly.'

'If by the remotest possibility I took you up on this offer how do I know that you wouldn't do a Jack on me?'

'Jack and I have different values when it comes to that sort of thing.'

'You can have no idea how it felt to know someone you trusted could behave so badly.'

The bell in the church tower struck a quarter past the hour. Alice shivered as the sun went behind a cloud and the Tao attendants laughed as their silk costumes fluttered, stirred by the sudden stiff breeze.

'Actually I do,' Mike said quietly.

'Our father misappropriated our mother's estate. He probably thought he was acting for the best but things didn't work out as he planned. Venetia's husband Tony was in poor health and,' Mike swallowed, 'he signed papers my father put before him without reading them properly.

'I'm afraid my father abused his trust. To his credit I think it was something my father later regretted but the damage was done.'

'Mike, I had no idea.'

'Venetia's been trying to make it up to us ever since, even though it wasn't her fault. If it hadn't been for our grandmother I don't know what would have happened.' Mike lowered his eyes and looked down at the grass.

'As a family we put on a united front but the wounds went deep.'

'I am so sorry.'

'Poor old Jack has been trying to put things right, like Venetia, but,' he shrugged, 'he doesn't have much of a business head on his shoulders.'

'He did one good deal,' Alice pointed out, 'with his finance company.'

'Can you find it in your heart to forgive him?'

'I already have.' Alice felt a load lift off her shoulders. 'And I sort of understand why you always stuck up for Jack. He was trying to do his best.'

'Then you'll think about Venetia's proposal?'

'I'm not making any promises.'

'David and Netta would approve.'

'What's it got to do with them?'

'I don't know ... I thought we might possibly follow their example.'

'What example?' Alice swallowed down the lump clogging her throat.

'Commitment?'

Mike had made an attempt to tame his dishevelled hair but it seemed to have inherited the Preston family trait of not following the rules.

His deep blue eyes were fixed on Alice and she knew she could no longer ignore the truth she had been so reluctant to acknowledge.

She had never been in love with Jack. He had been fun and she would always be fond of him but her relationship with Mike had shown her a new depth of feeling.

'Are you proposing marriage?' she asked.

At that moment a ping from Mike's mobile indicated an incoming text.

'It's from Jack,' he announced.

'What does he want now?' Alice stifled her irritation.

'He wants to know if you said yes.'

'You discussed the proposal with Jack?' Alice was outraged.

'I thought maybe he would say I was out of my mind to consider the idea. I mean he's the handsome go-getter of the family and you're,' Mike swallowed, 'brave and bold and beautiful.'

'What did Jack suggest you do?' Alice asked in a slow voice.

'He suggested I go for it.'

'Then why don't you?'

'Hey,' Mike protested as Alice snatched his mobile out of his hands, 'what are you doing?'

'Texting Jack to tell him I said yes.'

The mobile slipped out of her hands and into the long grass as Mike swept her up in his arms.

'Jack can wait, I can't.'

At the sight of Mike embracing Alice, the Tao assistants bowed happily to each other.

'Glad they didn't take as long as we did.' Netta linked arms with David. 'Come on. Let's leave them to it. They'll come to the party when they are ready.'

'My blessings on you both.' David bowed in their direction then followed Netta across the grass towards the marquee.

FESTIVAL FEVER
LOVE WILL FIND A WAY
HUNGRY FOR LOVE
ISLAND MAGIC
THE EIGHTH CHILD
CASTLE OF FLOWERS

We do hope that you have enjoyed reading this large print book.

Did you know that all of our titles are available for purchase?

We publish a wide range of high quality large print books including:
Romances, Mysteries, Classics
General Fiction
Non Fiction and Westerns

Special interest titles available in large print are:
The Little Oxford Dictionary
Music Book, Song Book
Hymn Book, Service Book

Also available from us courtesy of Oxford University Press:
Young Readers' Dictionary
(large print edition)
Young Readers' Thesaurus
(large print edition)

For further information or a free brochure, please contact us at:
Ulverscroft Large Print Books Ltd.,
The Green, Bradgate Road, Anstey,
Leicester, LE7 7FU, England.
Tel: (00 44) **0116 236 4325**
Fax: (00 44) **0116 234 0205**

Other titles in the
Linford Romance Library:

SAVING ALICE

Gina Hollands

Naomi Graham is the best family lawyer in the country. But beneath her professional demeanour lies a broken heart. When the man who caused that heartache — billionaire ex-husband Toren Stirling — returns to her life after a ten-year absence, Naomi doesn't want to know. Their painful struggle to start a family tore their relationship apart, so when Toren reveals that he has a young daughter, Alice, it comes as a shocking blow. Not only that, but he's now fighting a custody battle — and needs Naomi's legal expertise to help him win.

FLIGHT TO LOVE

Penny Oates

It's 1975, and starry-eyed air hostess Anthea is about to embark on her first international flight. An incident on the way to the airport — involving her car, an icy road and an irksome gentleman — leaves Anthea slightly dishevelled, but little does she know what drama still awaits her, both in the skies and in exotic Thailand. Against her better judgement, she falls under the spell of aristocratic Captain Sebastian Orly — and incurs the wrath of super-efficient yet standoffish senior stewardess Zara Vine, who happens to have designs on him herself . . .

THE ARTISTS OF WOODBRIDGE

Jean M. Long

Isla Milne intends to stay with her relatives in Woodbridge only until she has put her life back in order. But then she meets a group of local artists, amongst them talented sculptor Jed Rowley. Soon she becomes integrated in village life and involved with the summer school at Rowley Grange, and things take on an interesting dimension as she builds new and discovers old connections in the area. Meanwhile, Isla finds herself becoming increasingly attracted to Jed — but he is already dating the glamourous and possessive Nicole . . .

THE LION-TAMER'S DAUGHTER

Henriette Gyland

When her family's circus is disbanded and her beloved lion Rexus moved to a private menagerie in Norfolk, Justine volunteers to spend a few weeks settling him in. Arriving at the stately home, she receives mixed reactions from the residents. Lady of the house Priscilla is aloof, while her two daughters seem just a little too curious about the lion. But groundsman Tom's welcome is warm, and as the two grow closer, can Justine keep everyone safe until it's time for her to leave and start a new life elsewhere?